FRIENDS

DECEPTION & MURDERS

IN ARUBA

<u>**Other books by Steven Winer**</u>

Deception

Lies, Larceny & Lawyers

Brothers Law and Greed

Family Betrayal & Murder

Friends Greed & Murder

FRIENDS

DECEPTION & MURDERS
IN ARUBA

STEVEN WINER

Library of Congress Control Number: 2023913346
ISBN: Softcover 979-8-3694-0361-7
eBook 979-8-3694-0360-0

Print information available on the last page.

Rev. date: 07/28/2023

To order additional copies of this book, contact:
Xlibris
844-714-8691
www.Xlibris.com
Orders@Xlibris.com
854775

CONTENTS

Chapter 1 1
Chapter 2 15
Chapter 3 23
Chapter 4 32
Chapter 5 42
Chapter 6 51
Chapter 7 59
Chapter 8 67
Chapter 9 74
Chapter 10 80
Chapter 11 89
Chapter 12 96
Chapter 13 103
Chapter 14 110
Chapter 15 116
Chapter 16 123
Chapter 17 132
Chapter 18 138
Chapter 19 144
Chapter 20 151
Chapter 21 159
Chapter 22 164
Chapter 23 172
Chapter 24 181

Dear Reader:

I am apologizing before you begin to read this book concerning several grammar and spelling mistakes that you may encounter. No matter how many eyes look at the text of the book before publishing, mistakes are still made. I have found this in several other books I have read. Otherwise, despite these errors, please enjoy the read.

Steven Winer

CHAPTER 1

Johm Ruiz, a 45 year old native of Aruba, was lying dead on a cold stainless steel slab in a windowless first floor room inside the police station located just outside downtown Oranjestad, Aruba. The room was primarily used as storage for servers and computers by the police for the Caribbean Country Island. It was the only room that had central air conditioning. That was for a good reason. Its secondary use was as a morgue. All other rooms, on the first floor had window air conditioners. The police station was a large two story contemporary cement and concrete block building retaining the old traditional Dutch architectural style.

Aruba had always appreciated its Dutch culture. Since 1845 Aruba was part of the Kingdom of the Netherlands. It became independent in 1986, but continued to retain much of its Dutch background, culture and legal system. In 1990, the Aruban people voted, by a vast majority, to go back to a constitute country of the Netherlands. However, with the Netherland's blessings, all internal affairs and laws were still governed by the Aruban government with all political positions voted on by the Aruban people. The perfect compromise for the Island's nickname, "One Happy Island."

Doctor Jan Fingal, the part time coroner for the Island, was cleaning Ruiz's body preparing him for an autopsy. Dr. Fingal was in private practice, as a thoracic surgeon, associated with the Island's main hospital, Dr. Horacio Oduber Hospital. He was born on the Island but, with his family's blessings and their money, he received his undergraduate degree and medical degree at the University of Virginia. He did his internship at Walter Reed Hospital in Washington DC.

That's where Jan met his wife, Sally. She was a certified public accountant working at a small accounting firm. With the blessings of both families, they married in Washington DC after his internship was completed and they moved to Aruba. At first, it was a culture shock for Sally, but she adapted well. Jan helped her gain employment with the hospital where he worked. When Jan opened his private practice, Sally became his receptionist, bookkeeper and tax consultant. It worked out well for both of them. Dr. Fingal's background and medical reputation as a thoracic surgeon was the reason the Aruban authorities contracted with him to perform autopsies, whenever the law required one.

Dr. Fingal, as most other individuals was not perfect. But due to his position on the Island, he kept his vices as private as possible. As the appointed coroner, his responsibilities were to investigate all unnatural deaths, or deaths where the attending medical doctor was unable to emphatically state a cause of death. He was required to establish a positive identity of the deceased, determine the place, date, time, cause and classification of death. There had been few autopsies performed in that room. Dr. Fingal was delighted about that since he received no compensation for his government work. However, most of his closest friends, family and colleagues were under the impression that he was working for the government much more often than he actually admitted. This gave him time for his most expensive vice. One that he attempted to hide from Sally, but she never admitted that she was aware that he enjoyed gambling. After all, she ran his finances. She made sure it never got out of hand.

The fact that Dr. Fingal bragged about his government work seemed odd to many, since Aruba's murder and suspicious death rate was one of the lowest in the world. The last infamous murder was in 2005 when Natalee Holloway, a 17 year old senior, on her class trip with 124 other seniors, from Alabama's Mountain Brook High School, disappeared. Her body was never recovered. No autopsy was ever performed in that case. A gratification for Dr. Fingal's predecessor at the time, considering the world wide attention in that case.

Johm Ruiz was well known throughout the Island. He was one of the deputy custom officers for the Island. He supervised over 65 people who processed all of the local custom laws at the Queen Beatrix Airport and all other ports of entry for the Island. His death was a shock to all of the employees who worked with him, as well as many residents on the Island. Through his work he met many interesting people from all over the world. Some, who came to the Island frequently, he even befriended. Johm called them his 'frequent flyers'. Several of those frequent flyers invited him out to dinner and even had him come to their timeshare or hotel for cocktails and dinner.

One of his frequent flyers, Dr. Burton Woodcock, a physician who lived in Minneapolis, Minnesota, even invited him to his home back in the States. Ruiz took up his offer one time and enjoyed the culture and beauty of the City of Minneapolis, known as the City of Lakes. That was his one and only trip outside of Aruba during his life. Other frequent flyers were also very generous to Johm. That generosity, at certain times, initiated Ruiz to overlook certain required duty payments when going through customs. However, that didn't happen often enough for his superiors to notice. He never thought of it as corruption. Just a favor for a friend.

Johm's supervisor, Coy Dirks, reported him missing when he didn't show up, at the airport, for his regular shift at 9:30 AM, September 18, 2022. Other than his approved time off, Johm hadn't missed a day in twelve years. Ruiz lived alone after him and his wife, Natasha, divorced six years prior. His only child, a daughter, Kaydra, was attending college at the University of Florida. Ruiz wanted her to have a wide-ranging American education. It was very expensive for a government employee, but Ruiz had worked it out, in several different ways, to make sure his daughter's education was fully paid.

When he didn't show up for work and couldn't be reached by phone, the police were dispatched to his home. He was found lying lifeless on the floor in his kitchen. Nothing seemed out of place and there was no visible signs of a break in. There was no blood anywhere and the only strange visible mark on his body was a small bruise on his forehead. The police immediately believed it must have been a heart attack. He probably hit his head on something when he fell. However, with an overabundance of caution, the police sealed off his home as a possible crime scene until the local coroner viewed the body. Both his girlfriend, Alle Thiel, and his daughter had been notified by the Chief of Police, Biob Peterson. The Chief was also good friends with Johm and his ex-wife, Natasha, so, unbeknownst to anyone else, he also notified her. She was living in North Carolina. She left the Island immediately after their divorce was final. That seemed strange to many of their friends.

Islanders wondered. Was his death actually a medical occurrence or some sort of accident? Or, could have he been murdered? Even the unsophisticated Island police officers on scene couldn't determine that question. So, the Police Chief thought an autopsy was necessary. Once the crime scene tape went up on Ruiz's home, the Island's rumor mill was immediately in full intensity.

At 7:30 the morning after Ruiz's death, Bob and Kelly Walker were lounging on their balcony on the top floor of the Aruba Marriott Hotel & Casino. The hotel was located in the 'high rise' region of the Island as part of the exclusive Palm Beach area overlooking the Caribbean Sea. The views were breath taking from the eighth floor. They were both sipping on mimosas prior to going to the private dining room for breakfast. Both Bob and Kelly enjoyed their Champaign, especially the expensive brands.

The hotel made sure all their eighth floor guests had full access to their favorite libations. The private floor was known as the Tradewinds level. It was exclusively for adults with access to a private dining room for all their meals, including afternoon tea, which was a Netherlands tradition. Also, available all day were snacks, beer, wine, juices and water. After 6:00 PM, appetizers, including an abundance of sushi, and a fully stocked bar was available as a curtesy. Dinner started at 7:00 PM. The guests had the option of pouring their own drinks, just to their liking. Each top floor guest would request the brands of liquor, beer, wine or champagne of their choice. The private dining room was available between the hours of 7:00 AM and 9:00 PM every day, seven days a week.

There was also a private beach area for the Tradewinds guests. There were hotel employees designated for this area to make sure each guest maintained their privacy. Each guest had their own palapas, which was an open tiki hut whose roof was made out of dried palm fronds for shade. Each palapas had reclining lounges, towels and the availability of a multitude of drinks all day.

All other hotel guest had access only to the public beach areas. However, there was also four other lavish restaurants, several unique bars, two large pools and many diverse shops with various sundries and exclusive clothing and jewelry. The hotel also had the largest casino on the Island which was open 24 hours every day, 365 days a year. So, all guests not occupying the top floor were also treated very well.

While Bob was enjoying his mimosa he was scanning the daily newspaper, Aruba Today, the only English newspaper on the Island. He came across a story about the death of Johm Ruiz.

"Honey, you need to see this," exclaimed Bob. "Johm Ruiz died yesterday. There seems to be rumors that there may have been foul play."

"Foul play? How could that be? He was beloved by the custom employees and tourists. I remember when some doctor from Minneapolis, who was a frequent flyer like us, invited Johm to Minneapolis and took him to dinner at Charlie's Steak House in downtown Minneapolis. One of the best restaurants in town. Johm talked to us about it during several of our trips as we went through customs. Nice man. Do you remember? Johm always handled that doctor's entry and exit through customs, just like us. I can't believe that anyone would have any reason to harm him."

"The article says that his girlfriend, Alle Theil, is upset about the autopsy. She is adamant that it had to be a medical issue. She says most Islanders knew and loved the man. His daughter attends the University of Florida. I wonder how he could afford that. We need to speak with Harrison about this and find out what he may know about what really happened."

Kelly replied, "I don't think that would be necessary. We should just let the police handle the matter. Harrison has enough to do running this hotel and casino. Don't bother him with a police matter. Johm has a girlfriend and daughter. They can take care of whatever is needed."

Bob thought that remark to be unusual for Kelly, but he just let it go.

Harrison Ramsey was the overall General Manager of the Aruba Marriott Hotel & Casino. He had held that position for over seven years. He was born in Minneapolis, Minnesota and received his Bachelor and Masters degree in hospitality management from the University of Minnesota. He was hired by Marriott International, Inc. right out of school. He worked in several positions at various Marriott hotels including its subsidiary hotels in several states for 5 years before he was promoted to his current position in Aruba. He was still single since he moved around the Country and worked 80 hours a week. He didn't have a chance to settle down and get married. However he came close to asking several women, but he never actual was able to work that out. None of them wanted to move around the Country every several years.

Harrison and Bob Walker grew up together in Minneapolis and went to the same high school. They had been best friends for years. Both attended the University of Minnesota and pledged the same fraternity. Bob Walker majored in Business Administration and received his Masters Degree from the Carlson Business School at the University. Harrison actually introduced Bob to Kelly during their junior year while they were undergraduates. Kelly's parents and Harrison's parents were good friends. Kelly was attending St. Thomas University in St. Paul, Minnesota studying Business Administration. Bob and Kelly immediately hit it off and started dating. They married three years after they met. Harrison was Bob's best man at the wedding. It was always obvious to Harrison that Kelly wore the pants in that family. Bob was very easy going. Sometimes too easy. Kelly was always the aggressive one.

Once Harrison was promoted to his present managerial position in Aruba, it became the catalyst for Bob and Kelly to start vacationing there. They fell in love with the Island. The eighth floor of the Marriott was the cherry on the ice cream for the Walkers. Harrison's connections always gave the Walkers a very good rate. One that they couldn't pass. Over the years, Harrison started communicating more with Kelly than with Bob. That never upset Bob, but it made him wonder. The three of them still were very tight. But Kelly's ambitions were more on track with Harrison's than her husband's.

Alle Theil and Johm Ruiz had been seeing each other for over two years. Alle was 15 years younger than Johm. She was born in International Falls, Minnesota, a small city located on the Canadian border. After graduating from International Falls High School, she wanted to escape from that small town as soon as possible. Her parents and two brothers loved the town, but Alle wanted a lot more than what her parents had, or, what the town could offer her in terms of employment and men. Her brothers and father were hunters and fisherman, but Alle wanted to be more cosmopolitan. Her father worked at the Boise Cascade paper mill, as did 60% of the rest of town. The winters were brutal and could last nearly 9 months. Alle hated it.

So after graduation, Alle moved to Minneapolis and attended The Minneapolis Metropolitan College and received her Associates degree in social work. It was a two year course of study. She found it difficult to find a job, both in private practice and governmental health facilities since she only had the two year degree. However, there was a growing community of Somali Muslims moving into the Cedar-Riverside neighborhood in downtown Minneapolis near the Minneapolis campus of the University of Minnesota. Alle decided to go out on her own and rent a small office in that area.

That area became known to the people of Minneapolis as 'Little Mogadishu'. Alle signed a two year lease to start her own practice. Her landlord was an offshore limited liability company. A Somali real estate agent handled the negotiations for the lease on behalf of the owner. Alle counseled a few of the younger unmarried Somali woman who were interested in assimilating into Minneapolis society and eventually moving out of 'Little Mogadishu'.

That venture lasted for less than 2 months due to a challenging language barrier, resistance from the fathers of many of the young women she counseled and the difficulty of getting paid for her work. She eventually started running out of money. Then her world changed.

One afternoon four Somali men came into her office. The oldest of the four men was wearing a T-shirt, jeans and Nike running shoes. He walked up to her desk and stood in front of her. He stared at her and said nothing. The other 3 men, wearing traditional Somali clothing, stood by the door blocking anyone from entering the room.

"May I help you sir?" uttered a scared Alle.

"Yes you can," said the man standing in front of her desk. "I don't allow women in my neighborhood to be encouraged by outsiders to leave this community. I understand that you are teaching English and the ways of the culture and laws of your Country. If I knew you were renting one of my offices to brainwash young Somali women, I would never have allowed you to rent this office. My rental agent should have informed me of your intentions when you signed your lease. As of today your lease is cancelled. Be out of here by the end of the day."

Alle was stunned. She had been in that office for just under 2 months and neither her landlord nor the real estate agent asked her about what kind of work she would be doing.

"My name is Diric Omar. I am the finance director for the local Mosque. I run 'Little Mogadishu'. Here is your compensation, from my company, to have you sign a release for your remaining obligations under the lease, including other matters to be determined, by me, in the future. Omar then handed Alle an envelope and a release for her to sign.

Alle had no idea what he meant about other future matters. But, she was not going to argue with this terrifying man. She was contemplating a way out of the lease anyway, due to her financial issues. Alle signed the release without even reading all of it. The Release included a statement of obligations to be fulfilled in the future, as dictated by Diric Omar. After she read the full Release, Alle had no idea what that meant.

"I don't want to see you in this office tomorrow or any other day. For this compensation you just received I will expect that you will do me a favor someday in the future when I contact you. I want you, Ms. Alle Thiel, to call the number on the front of the envelope. Ask for my assistant. His name is next to the number. Let him know where you are living. I don't want to have one of those men behind me attempt to find you. That would not turn out well for you or your family up North in that small border town. Do we understand each other?"

Alle looked in the envelope. There was ten thousand dollars in 100 dollar bills. She was shocked. There was a short lull while Alle was counting the money and she finally begrudgingly said, "I understand."

But she really didn't. Omar turned around and walked to the exit and left with the three security men following him. That was the most bizarre experience that Alle ever experienced. However, on the positive side, she was going to leave anyway. Now she had money to do something. What this favor was all about must have been some kind of threat, at least in Alle's mind. She thought he was just trying to scare her so she would leave. That he did very well.

Since the weather in Minneapolis could also be harsh during the winter months, Alle decided to take her new found money and get as far away from Minneapolis as possible. That day, and the last several months in "Little Mogadishu', was a strange experience. She never wanted to repeat it. So Alle decided to take a vacation, for an undetermined time, or until her money ran out, to the most distant warm Caribbean Island she could locate from Minneapolis. After looking at a map of the Caribbean, and reading brochures on different Caribbean resorts and Islands, she decided on Aruba. She read all about the Island. She was curious that Aruba was more of a dry desert Island verses the other usual tropical Island. That fascinated her. There Diric Omar would never find her. It was 4,000 miles from Minneapolis. The trip, along with her new found riches, would also give her time to ponder what she really wanted do with her life. She informed her mother as to what had happen and where she was going on vacation. All her mother could think about was Natalee Holloway. That frightened her. Alle told her mother that her investigation found that Aruba had one of the lowest crime rates, including very few murders. That was one of the reasons she picked that Island. Her mother understood, but was still worried.

While Alle vacationed on the Island, she frequented many of the establishments in the downtown Oranjestad entertainment district, just a few blocks from her hotel, the Aruba Radisson. She met many new people and spent some evenings with new 'friends'. Most of them were tourists from all over the world, but mostly the United States. One evening she decided that she wanted to see how the wealthy tourists vacationed. She decided to take a cab to the Marriott Hotel & Casino in the high rise area of the Island. All the expensive hotels, restaurants and clubs were located in the Palm Beach area. She loved the high rise hotel atmosphere, its décor and the hustle and bustle everywhere. The casinos was crowded and money was flowing everywhere she looked. At the Marriott, there was live music in both the lobby bar and the casino.

She decided to take a seat at the lobby bar. It was a huge, very modern, round bar in the middle of the lobby. It had at least three dozen comfortable stools around it. There were multiple tables, both high tops and low tables with furniture around them. All were in the bar area. When Alle found a stool at the bar, almost every stool was occupied. People were drinking expensive martinis and tropical drinks, laughing and having a good time. It was more of an older crowd than the downtown entertainment district. She liked that. There was a man by the bar high top tables with an electric guitar and computerized background music singing American rock & roll songs. It was alluring to Alle. Sitting next to her, at the bar, was a good looking older man drinking a martini.

Alle, who was not shy, turned to him and said, "My name is Alle, what's yours?"

Surprised by the woman's come on, he said, "My name is Johm. Johm Ruiz."

They chatted for over an hour while each had several drinks. Finally Johm asked Alle if she would like to go to dinner at one of the restaurants in the hotel. He had told her he lived on the Island and came to the hotel a few nights a week to relax after work. Also, he admitted being divorced. That comforted Alle who told him that she was single and on vacation. That night was the start of a two year relationship. Alle's family were shocked that a small town girl was spending her youth on a small Caribbean Island, over 4,000 miles away from Northern Minnesota. The communications between Alle and her family became less and less over time. Alle didn't miss Minnesota at all. She grew into the Island life easily.

Johm assisted Alle in finding a nice comfortable apartment just outside the city of Nood. That was only 10 minutes to the high rise district where Johm lived in a comfortable house with his daughter, Kaydra. Johm had been divorced for several years. With his many contacts it was easy for Johm to get Alle an intern position at a woman's health clinic where Alle could assist in counseling young women. No license was required in Aruba. Her two year degree was sufficient for her to obtain social work employment. The Island had very few counselling facilities. Her clinic was thrilled to have her.

Eventually, Johm and Alle started discussing marriage. However, he knew he would need the blessing of his daughter first. Johm and his daughter, Kaydra, were very close. From the first time Alle met Kaydra, they also got along well, even though she thought Alle may have been a little too young for her father. Kaydra left the Island to go to college sometime after her and Alle met. Johm and his ex-wife, Natasha, rarely spoke. Neither did Kaydra. It was an unscrupulous divorce.

When marriage discussions started, Kaydra was 16 years old and still living at home going to school. Her plans were to go to college at the University of Florida, majoring in hospitality management. She was also contemplating a Masters Degree with the hope of eventually working for one of the major hotels or resorts on Aruba. She loved living on the Island. Her father had to find a way to fund Kaydra's education. He too wanted her to work on the Island. Kaydra knew how much money her father made as a supervisor for a government agency. She wasn't sure how he could fund her education, which wasn't cheap. She thought that he must have been saving for many years. She knew her mother would never help her with her college expenses. She never even offered.

When Kaydra heard about her father's death she was a sophomore at the University of Florida. She was shattered. How could this happen to such a young man? Alle and Johm never did got married prior to his death. They just remained good friend and lived in their separate locations. Alle's relationship with Johm changed slowly as their discussions about marriage increased. Johm had changed. He started to yell at Alle more and accuse her of things she hadn't done.

Kaydra had to get back to Aruba as soon as possible when her father died. She desperately needed to know what happened. She also wanted to have input, along with Alle, concerning any final arrangements. Foul play was the last thought on her mind. That couldn't have happened to her father. Although, in her mind, her mother would be the only person she could think of who would wish bad will on her father. But Kaydra dismissed that thought quickly. After hearing from the police, Alle and Kaydra spoke on the phone and arrangements were made for Alle to pick Kaydra up at the airport when the 12:40 flight from Miami to Oranjestad landed the next day.

Dr. Fingal started the autopsy on Johm Ruiz within 18 hours after the police delivered the body to the morgue. No permission from the next of kin was necessary, under Aruba law, since neither Ruiz's internist nor Dr. Fingal could equivocally determine the cause of death. The first item in any autopsy was to determine with absolute assurance that the body was actually Johm Ruiz. Seemed senseless in this case since Dr. Fingal and Johm knew each other. But the doctor, as required, noted his height, weight, age, sex and any distinguishing characteristics such as birthmarks, scars, tattoos, etc. He also fingerprinted the body for positive identification in case they may be needed for a future police investigation.

Photographs were taken of the body with and without clothes. Any out of the ordinary marks on the body or his clothes were also observed and photographed. None appeared obvious. One never knows whether any droplets of blood, organic materials or any residues found on clothing may be helpful in a possible police investigation.

Of all of the preliminary items noted by the doctor while observing the corpse, was a fresh bruise or contusion on the left side of the body's forehead. Something or someone caused Ruiz's blood vessels to leak causing a purple and yellow tint to the skin. But no blood was found at the scene. The doctor determined the bruise to be a hematoma which would be caused by either a fall or someone hitting the forehead with a blunt instrument. X-rays were taken of the bruised area as well as other parts of the body to determine if there may be any broken or fractured bones.

Blood and tissue samples were extracted to be sent to the local lab in Curacao, the adjacent Island to Aruba, and just several miles away, for a full toxicology workup. Aruba didn't have facilities for a full toxicology workup. This workup was to determine if any drugs, alcohol or poisons were involved in the death. The results of the toxicology report would take about a week. But Dr. Fingal would wait a few days to send the blood and tissue to the lab to make sure his friends and colleagues thought his governmental work took up a lot of his time.

During that week he would go between the morgue and several hotel casinos to gamble. Only his wife was aware of what he was doing. Even the Chief of Police wasn't quite sure why certain autopsies took such a long time, but he was certain that his choice of Dr. Fingal as the Island's coroner was still the right choice. He thought that the doctor was extremely careful and diligent to make sure every conclusion was correct before signing a death certificate.

Dr. Fingal used a scalpel to open the body cavity for an examination of all of the major organs and bones in the body. The intestines, spleen and stomach were observed and samples of their contents and tissues were extracted to determine if there was any partially digested food. This was performed since it may be used to help determine a more exact time of death and where the body may have been prior to his death. Ruiz had cereal, milk, fruit and orange juice in his stomach. The doctor removed the top of the skull, so the brain could be observed, to help determine the extent of the bruise or contusion on the body's forehead.

Except for the discoloration of the left portion of the skull, nothing unusual was found during the preliminary autopsy. As Dr. Fingal was dictating his report, detectives George Franken and Esmar Geil, the lead detectives on the case, entered the room to discuss the autopsy with the doctor.

"So doc, what the hell happened to our good friend Johm?" asked lead detective Franken.

"George, I have no idea. Everything I observed on or in the body was normal for a middle aged male. I only observed a small bruise on the left side of his forehead. I can't tell if it was from an accidental fall or from foul play. Of course the toxicology report may take up to a week of so for a final determination of death."

"So what's your determination for purposes of the death certificate doc?"

"Unknown causes subject to further investigation by the police."

Detective Geil interrupted, "Shit. So this wasn't some kind of heart attack or seizure or something like that?"

"No, the man was in perfect health," said the doctor.

"So what was the time of death?" asked Detective Franken.

"Between 7:00 AM and 10:00 AM yesterday morning. September 18."

"So he might have had his last breakfast meal before he keeled over," said detective Geil.

"In fact he did. He had cereal, milk, fruit and orange juice."

"Well, what am I supposed to tell Johm's girlfriend and daughter as to when the body can be released for a proper funeral?"

"The body will be released after a review of the toxicology report, a further investigation by myself, and your further police investigation. Gentlemen, you know the drill."

"Investigation? We're not homicide detectives. We don't have extensive experience with this type of investigation."

Detective Geil interrupted again, "When that Holloway girl went missing, at least we had help from the Netherlands Police Corp and the FBI from the States. This one is going to be our responsibility. I hope the Chief understands that and gets us some help. The damn press is going to be all over this once they hear your conclusions Doc."

"Gentleman, my work is done here for today. I will do a more extensive investigation of the body in a day or two. Tell the girlfriend and daughter the body will be safe in our morgue until you have finished your investigation, the toxicology report is reviewed and I finalize the death certificate."

Detective Geil looked at his senior detective and unenthusiastically asked, "Okay George, where do we go from here?"

CHAPTER 2

Harrison Ramsey was on the phone, in his office, with Coy Dirksz, the Director of Immigration for the Aruba Government, when Bob Walker knocked on his door. Harrison waved Bob in as he was still talking on the phone. Bob could hear the end of Harrison's discussion with Coy about Ruiz's death.

"I am so sorry about Johm," said Harrison. "Let me know if the hotel can do anything for Johm's family. Keep in touch, please." Harrison then hung up the phone.

"What the Hell happened Harrison? Did Ruiz find out something about our little project?"

Harrison couldn't answer that question since he didn't find out any information about Ruiz's death from the Immigration department. Also, he was amazed at the fact that Bob called the scheme a little project. Kelly must not have trusted her own husband with the workings of the scheme. Strange, but very 'Kellyish'.

"Was Johm's death just a fluke accident or is something more going on that I need to know."

"Bob, just cool it. Let things play out. Coy knows nothing about Johm's death and has already related that fact to the authorities. It could have just been an accident."

"I don't believe in coincidences. Have you spoken with Irving yet?"

"No. Leave him out of this. I don't want any connections between you or me with Irving. Especially phone conversations. Phone records are the first item investigations rely on. Come on Bob, get it together.

You worry too much. Irving Wernet is a reliable person. He knows how to handle himself. We would have known from Irving, immediately, if anyone in immigration was even coming close to finding out anything."

Bob was not that convinced. An accident? Dr. Fingal was too efficient of a doctor to know whether or not an accident occurred. He could have detected that immediately. Why the autopsy? Now there's an investigation. Everything had been working so perfectly, or so thought Bob.

"OK, Harrison. When I get back to the States I'll have Kelly inform her connections to hold off until this 'business' with Ruiz is over."

"No Bob. I'll take care of it. Leave our connections out of this."

Harrison and Bob were very good friends who had known each other almost all their lives. Between the two of them, Harrison had always been the brains and Bob, who had good book smarts, but sad street smarts, would almost always go along with Harrison. However, Bob always had a panicky streak. Harrison had to accept that fact or they never would have stayed friends for so long. So Harrison agreed with Bob and he would make sure that everyone would hold off for a while. But Harrison knew that wasn't going to happen. Kelly was much better understanding the obstacles in their world than Bob. So Harrison would have a word with her when the time was right. For the meantime, operations with their 'little project' could never temporarily come to a halt.

George Franken and Esmar Geil decided that it would be prudent for them to go to Johm Ruiz's home and start their investigation there. On the way to the scene there were many unsaid words between the two detectives. Neither really knew where to start the investigation. Even Franken who was on the force for over 10 years had little experience in homicide matters. He had always followed the lead of the Netherlands police force or the FBI. This time they were on their own. Franken trusted that the NCB would still be at Ruiz's house. They hoped that they would point the detectives in the right direction. Both detectives were thinking the same thing but said nothing about it to each other.

The NCB, or National Central Bureau, was located in Aruba's capital city of Oranjestad. It was mostly a dedicated terrorism and safety unit for many of the Caribbean Islands. It also dealt with murders of governmental personnel, when necessary. The NCB were much more sophisticated than either Franken or Geil. Both detectives were counting on that sophistication in this matter.

The Caribbean was located on shipping routes linking the Americas, the Atlantic Ocean and the Caribbean Sea. This was an archipelago of 7,000 Islands which were challenging for local law enforcement to monitor. Over the last few years the Caribbean Islands were proving increasingly attractive to organized crime networks seeking a regional hub to engage in a multitude of serious crimes that the local law enforcement was not equipped to handle. These crimes included trafficking in firearms, people and counterfeit goods, in addition to money laundering and bulk cash smuggling. Murders of governmental workers were also included in their duties, such as customs agents like Johm Ruiz.

When the detectives arrived at Ruiz's home, Houston Cavey and Cyrus Turnbull, both former FBI agents, currently working for the NCB, were performing criminal investigative services for the detectives to determine what may have happened that morning of September 18. After all four men introduced themselves to each other and exchanged business cards, Houston Cavey informed the detectives that they would take whatever evidence they had obtained back to their downtown office, examine it, and give the detectives their report as soon as it was completed. Both detectives were enormously relieved. However, Houston was not very encouraging to the detectives since very little evidence, of any crime, was found. Both NCB operatives were relatively certain that no crime was committed at the home. There were various fingerprints, a smudge that may have looked like a small droplet of blood on the corner of the center island in the kitchen and some saliva on the floor. But nothing was said about those facts to the detectives.

"Our work is completed here detectives," said Houston. "We'll get back to you as soon as our report is complete. Otherwise the scene is now yours to examine."

As both of the NCB agents left, the detectives weren't quite sure where to begin. Esmar looked at George and asked him what he wanted him to do first.

"Just look around and see if there are any things out of place or if something may look unusual. Be a detective. Do some detecting."

Both George and Esmar were certainly out of their elements. It was truly the blind leading the blind. Both detectives were thinking that maybe the toxicology report or the NCB report would give them some clue as to how to try to resolve this case. But, again, nothing was said between them. Or maybe this wasn't a case at all. Esmar just started observing the scene while George called the Chief to give him an update.

Where they would go from there was an unknown. Luckily, the Chief was not in his office and George left a message with his assistant that they were working with the NCB and checking out Ruiz's home. George then told Esmar that they were going to the airport to interview Ruiz's fellow custom agents. Maybe they could ascertain who the last person was who saw Ruiz alive. Or, at least, find out if Ruiz went directly home after his last shift. Maybe someone heard Johm indicate that he was on his way somewhere else. Nothing else came to George's mind as to the next step in the investigation. Esmar said nothing.

Alle was at the airport, just outside customs waiting for Kaydra to arrive. When they saw each other, they both hugged and began to cry. Kaydra wanted to go to the mortuary and see her father. But Alle told her that her father's body was still locked in the morgue until the toxicology report was completed. Kaydra didn't understand.

"Why is my father still in the morgue? I thought he died of some disease, or a heart attack. Is there some evidence that he may have been murdered? I need to know."

"I don't know. I am as confused as you are. I called Dr. Fingal, who knows some of my friends, but, he wouldn't tell me anything. I tried to call the police, but I was told that a detective would come by and speak with me in a day or two."

"So what am I supposed to do? Who do I talk to? Where do I go?"

"You can stay with me until we get to the bottom of this crazy matter. Your father's house is currently a crime scene, so you can't go there. But, trust me, we'll get to the bottom of this tomorrow. Just stay with me tonight. We can talk about this tragedy and try to make some sense of it."

After Harrison and Bob's conversation, Harrison contacted Kelly and asked if she could come to his office and have a chat. Harrison was concerned that Bob was getting nervous about their responsibilities. Johm Ruiz's death had panicked Bob. Harrison felt that he needed to be reassured that this incident wouldn't lead back to any of the participants in their lucrative undertaking. Kelly was the person to handle that issue.

Kelly had always been the bond that had kept Bob daring with all of the other participants in their scheme. A little pep talk between Kelly and Bob would go a long way to keep the undertaking under control. Harrison was certain of that.

When Bob went to the beach that morning to arrange for their palapa, Kelly went to Harrison's office.

"What did you need to talk to me about?" Asked Kelly.

"Haven't you seen Bob's attitude change since Ruiz's death?"

"Not really. He is always a little nervous from time to time. Ruiz's death didn't cause much of a difference, maybe a little rant with a few questions as to how he died. But I told him that I had no knowledge as to what happened to Ruiz," admitted Kelly. "He didn't make a more extensive inquiry about who may had been involved?"

"Bob did cross examine me a little to try to find out if I knew something, but nothing much different than when any other incident would occur."

"This isn't just a little incident, Kelly, this is serious. I know you have an idea what happened. You're smart enough to have figured this out. But I was concerned that you may have discussed your thoughts with Bob."

"Give me a break, Harrison. Bob knows that we have a few thousand dollars in our safe. But he is unaware of the half million dollars cash hidden somewhere else in our hotel room. He may know that there is some more money somewhere else, but has no idea where or how much. Even if I discussed my thoughts on Ruiz, Bob would be cool about it. But, be assured, I said nothing since I know nothing."

"Kelly, I am a little concerned about Bob. I love the guy. He's my best friend, but he just doesn't have your temperament in these matters. Everyone is looking to you to make sure he stays composed and natural during your trips to Aruba. The last thing we want is for the authorities to suspect anything due to something Bob may accidently say or do. Remember it was only you and me and Marc Harper who were to know about this scheme."

Kelly was a little offended by Harrison's accusations toward her husband. After all they have known each other for over 30 years. He should have been giving him some slack. However, the scheme that they were all now involved in had become substantial and dangerous. Kelly knew her husband was a little over his head. When the operation was small, Bob was really into the deceptions of the operation. It was actually fun as well as a little lucrative. But things have escalated, and maybe Kelly was beginning to understand Harrison's point.

"OK, friend. Maybe Bob is a little nervous, but trust me. I'll handle him."

"I knew you would see it my way. I love you guys and I'm glad you would see it my way. Let's make sure we keep in touch."

Kelly acquiesced, and left to go meet her husband at the beach. She, however, left that conversation with a lot of questions she didn't want to ask. How did Ruiz really die? Did Harrison have something to do with it? Did Ruiz somehow find out something concerning their scheme? After all, he was a supervisor for customs. Did he overhear or see something between Irving and her or Bob when they arrived in Aruba this trip? She should have asked those questions. But deep in her gut she really didn't want to know the answers.

Bob and Kelly enjoyed palapa number 1. It was the closest to the beach and they loved to interact with people as they walked the beach. Most of the people they spoke with were tourists. They would give recommendations about restaurants, tours and nightclubs. People were very appreciative. Bob and Kelly enjoyed informing people about all of the things to see and do on the Island. But also, some of the people that walked that beach may have been part of their scheme. Many transfers of money and goods occurred, in plain sight, on that beach. Kelly had no idea which transfers were involved. She was unaware of everyone who had been recruited by Omar. She was always told it was on a need to know basis.

"What took you so long to get here?" asked Bob.

"I needed to go to the sundry store. I was out of some make up and mouthwash. I took it back to our room. Sorry about that." Kelly lied.

Bob didn't even give it another thought.

About an hour later a familiar man, known to Kelly as Brad Nickolas but known to Bob only as John Smith, was walking the beach. He started to approach Bob. He was wearing only a bathing suit, a Chicago Cubs baseball cap and water shoes He had a small satchel hung over his shoulder. He took the satchel off his shoulder and asked Bob to hand it to him.

"I'm sorry sir," Bob said, "Are you John Smith? And what is it exactly you want from me?"

Brad gave Bob a perplexed look and then turned to Kelly and uttered very softly, "You better give it to me Bitch, you know the routine."

"I'm sorry sir, you must have the wrong person. I have no idea what you are talking about," again said Bob as he looked at Kelly.

Bob was certain that Harrison had temporarily called off the scheme as they had discussed in his office. But maybe Mr. Smith didn't get the message yet.

Brad then grabbed Kelly's left arm and squeezed it hard and again softly uttered, "Don't play any games with me. You better give it to me or there will be consequences."

When Bob saw Kelly's confrontation with Mr. Smith, he immediately came to her rescue and separated the two.

"Move on sir, or the consequences will be on you," said Bob.

John Smith, or whatever his real name was, looked very angry, but let go of Kelly's arm and slowly walked away. He gave Kelly a look that made the hair on the back of her neck elevate. She was really scared. Unusual for Kelly, but it made her think hard about what was really happening.

Bob looked at Kelly and said, "What the Hell was that?"

Kelly, who was still terrified, told Bob in a calm manner that she would tell him about it when they got back to their room. Until then she pleaded to just move on like that incident never happened. Bob looked confused and scared, but took Kelly's hint and tried to relax and just go on with his day. Little, at the time, did either of them know the true consequences of that encounter.

CHAPTER 3

Kelly knew that at some time that day she needed to speak with Harrison and let him know what happened on the beach. Kelly made a dinner reservation for her, Bob and Harrison at the hotel's main restaurant, Ruth's Chris Steak House. The reservation was in a private booth in the back of the restaurant for 9:00 that evening. By mentioning Harrison's name as one of the diners, it assured the most private booth in the restaurant.

Kelly, like most of the participants in the scheme, didn't know all, or even how many participants were involved. Only a very few of the top participants knew everything that was actually taking place in half a dozen locations in the US and the Caribbean. Harrison was but one of the participants of what he believed to be only a scheme by an organization from Minneapolis. At least that is what he told Kelly. That also made Kelly question Harrison's knowledge of the scheme. Maybe he knew more than he was telling her? But why? What did Harrison really know? Kelly was smart and she vowed to find out the truth. Kelly had only a partial knowledge of the scheme. She knew that she was missing some of the workings of the undertaking.

She, with some assistance from Bob had a certain role to perform. She did her part well. The intrigue was invigorating to Kelly, and the money, even though not a lot, was getting a little better every month. As far as Kelly knew, no one was even close to finding out the totality of the scheme. But due to the incident on the beach that afternoon, she had to confront Harrison for more information. The risk was starting to get more perilous. She had no idea that a transfer of funds was to take place that morning. Was there a communication failure or was it on purpose?

Bob's only knowledge of the undertaking was that Harrison was allegedly skimming some of the hotel and casino's income. He and his wife's task was to hold the money until Harrison could launder it through several of his contacts in Aruba. Bob was not an official participant in the scheme and was oblivious to the vastness of it. Kelly made sure of that. Then the incident on the beach, and most disturbing, Johm Ruiz's sudden death. That triggered something inside Bob that made him believe that there had to be more to what was really happening. Hence his reaction when he confronted Harrison.

Also, when he witnessed the man, known to him only as John Smith, nearly accosting his wife on the beach, again he knew there had to be more to what was actually going on. Bob's only option was to ask Kelly if she was hiding something from him. He hoped that wasn't the case. But, obviously Harrison trusted Kelly more with handling the disbursements of money over his best friend. Bob, however, now needed to know what was really happening. Luckily the three of them were having dinner that evening. Maybe that would be the time to bring up Bob's concerns? But with the death of Johm Ruiz, Kelly wasn't so sure that Harrison would, or even could, give them the answers they both so desperately wanted. The three of them had eaten together hundreds of times over the years and they all got along famously. But this dinner was going to be different. That frightened Kelly and made her think twice about the upcoming evening.

A couple of hours before their scheduled dinner, Harrison was making his rounds at the hotel. He entered the casino and immediately went to the "high roller" area to welcome his most profitable customers. There at the $100.00 blackjack table Harrison noticed Dr. Jan Fingal. He was the only player at that table. It was a little early for all of the wealthy "high rollers". He was, however, one of Harrison's frequent flyers, as he called them.

The doctor loved to gamble. However, the well liked doctor usually lost a little more than he could afford. At least at the Marriott's casino. Harrison had given the doctor a small line of credit of $25,000.00 and didn't ask for any cash up front. Harrison knew that Fingal was good for that amount. He made a lot of money in his profession. It was one of the doctor's secrets he kept from the rest of the world. Harrison agreed to do the same. The locals very seldom gambled. If they did, it was at one of the lower class hotel small casinos, and for much smaller sums. So the extent of his addiction was known to only a few on the Island. Harrison being one of them. The locals didn't think Jan had any kind of addiction. They just thought he enjoyed a little gambling here and there.

"Hello Jan," as the doctor looked up and saw Harrison. "How are you doing tonight?"

"I'm down just a little, but the night is young."

Harrison looked at the dealer and asked him how much was a little?

"Oh, about $5,000.00."

"Doctor, I believe you must owe this casino close to six figures already," whispered Harrison. "You know your line of credit is only $25,000.00. I have let you go because I knew you would be good for it, but I hate to be confronted by the home office about this."

The doctor was busy playing cards and didn't even hear Harrison. Fingal looked at the two cards he was just dealt face up. It was an ace and a four. His $500.00 bet was laying just above those cards.

"See Harrison, my luck is starting to change," as he placed another $500.00 worth of chips down and told the dealer he was doubling down and to give him one card only.

The dealer had a six showing over his one turned down card. The doctor was sure the dealer had a face card or a ten under his six. Surely the dealer would break and Jan would win a thousand dollars. The dealer dealt Dr. Fingal his one card. It was the Queen of Hearts. That gave the doctor a total of 15.

The dealer then turned over his hidden card and it was a ten. The doctor guessed correctly. The dealer had sixteen. Blackjack rules are simple. The dealer must always deal himself cards so long as the dealer had 16 or less. If the dealer had 17 or more, the dealer was required to stand. Since the dealer had 16, he was required to draw another card. Fingal was sure the dealer would deal himself a high card and be over 21. The dealer dealt himself the next card and it was a five giving the dealer 21. Dr. Fingal lost another $1000.00.

Harrison just watched and said nothing as the dealer took the doctor's $1000.00 worth of chips. Fingal then put down another $500.00 for the next hand.

"Shouldn't you be going home to your family doctor?"

"Just a few more hands Harrison. I'm sure my luck will change."

"Jan, I can only do so much for you. I have bosses you know. You are way over your line of credit. I can forgive your current losses tonight and your other outstanding debt if you just go home now."

"You know Harrison, I just spoke with the company finalizing the toxicology tests on Johm Ruiz. I know you and Johm may be more than just friends. Maybe you and he have something going for your frequent flyers at customs?"

Harrison gently grabbed the doctor's collar and pulled him out of his chair and gently pushed him back from the table so as to not make a scene.

"God Damit Fingal. You know better than to mention Ruiz to me in public. I agreed to cancel your debt. I can only cover what you currently have outstanding before questions are asked of me. You don't want that to happen. Your reputation is too important to you. So why don't you go home to your family now just like I asked you."

"Ok Harrison. I just thought my luck was about to change."

"Get out of here Jan before I call security"

"Okay, okay. Don't get so prissy. I'll get you some money in a few weeks. I'll pay the hotel upfront some money to make it look right on your books. If I take too much out of my account at one time my wife gets suspicious. Unfortunately I hired her as my book keeper for my practice. Big mistake."

"I don't give a damn about your wife, just leave. And keep your mouth shut. I don't know what you know about Ruiz, but just keep your mouth shut."

Dr. Fingal gave a smile to Harrison and walked out of the casino to his car. Fingal knew he had hit a nerve with Harrison when he mentioned Ruiz. Harrison followed him to the casino door and made sure he drove away. Harrison knew about Fingal's gambling compulsion, but Fingal was the Island's only coroner. He knew he would finalize Ruiz's autopsy. Harrison thought that cancellation of up to a $100,000.00 credit at his casino would be sufficient for Harrison to get Fingal to alter the toxicology report. But Harrison quickly found out that compulsive gamblers are hard to control. As he went back to his rounds, before meeting Bob and Kelly for dinner, he cussed himself out for getting involved with Fingal. He hoped he wouldn't be any more of a problem. Harrison could hide the doctor's losses only for so long. Otherwise he would have to be dealt with and that would become a larger problem.

The real mystery was the fact that Harrison wasn't even sure what happened to Johm Ruiz. Harrison just assumed his death was foul play, but he really had not been given any information about the situation. Harrison was just covering for any contingency that may occur in the scheme. After all, Ruiz was not the only custom agent that checked Bob and Kelly Walker and Brad Nickolas through customs when they were both coming in and leaving Aruba. Harrison was also aware of Irving. Brad had told Harrison that Irving was the custom man Omar okayed for the scheme. But Harrison started to believe that Johm Ruiz must have also been involved in the scheme as a backup at customs. No one had told him about Ruiz, not even Brad. Someone else involved may have recruited Ruiz. That was not unusual. But, Harrison felt he needed to protect his friends Bob and Kelly first and foremost.

Harrison's other problem was Irving Wernet. As second in line to the Director of Immigration for the Island, Harrison knew that the police would be interviewing him about Ruiz's death. Harrison had spoken with Irving after he and Bob had their discussion that morning. Irving was calm and indicated that he had heard Kelly and Johm talking about what was in her suit case when they came to the Island this trip. During a break, Irving mentioned that conversation to Johm and was curious as to what that was about. Johm attempted to sluff it off as idle conversation with a frequent visitor and good friends, but Irving wasn't sure he bought that explanation. He wanted to know if something irregular was going on. Irving was aware of Kelly and Bob's frequent trips to Aruba and acted as if he knew there was nothing suspicious. Even Irving didn't know if Johm was involved.

Harrison didn't want to reveal that he knew that Irving was working with Brad. Irving had some idea that Johm may have been a part of the money laundering scheme. However, Irving really liked Johm and couldn't believe he would be part of any kind of scheme. He was an honest manager for customs. However, he did need money to pay for his daughter's education.

Almost every time Kelly and Bob came to the Island, Johm now would handle their customs entry. Johm nor Irving didn't usually handle many custom entries or do many searches. That was very unusual in Irving's mind. So once in a while Irving, without Johm's knowledge, would handle Bob and Kelly's entry through customs. When Irving did that, there was never any mention of money. But Irving never checked their luggage either. He just let them go through customs. Irving was involved but had no idea what was actually happening. In Irving's mind, Bob and Kelly were just nice frequent flyers who loved the Island. Irving also had no idea as to any involvement in any illegal matters by Johm. That just wasn't his nature. Brad liked it that Irving had told Harrison, several days ago, that something needed to be done before Johm did any more investigating or maybe did something even more stupid.

On the other hand, Johm never thought that Irving could be a part of the scheme. But everyone involved wasn't aware of all of the people Brad engaged. It was on a need to know basis. Harrison told Irving to handle it, but to handle it quietly. The fact that Johm turned up dead surprised and even frightened Harrison. But Harrison didn't ask if Irving was involved, or even if he knew something about the incident. But, in the back of his mind he was confused. Something went wrong. Maybe both Irving and Johm were involved in the scheme, but Harrison didn't know that. Omar and Brad were strict about telling people as to who was or wasn't involved. Did Irving find out about Johm? Why the scheme was being perpetrated in that manner was very strange to all participating.

Something else must have been going on. However, Harrison wasn't worried about that part of the scheme.

The morning after Kaydra arrived in Aruba, she and Alle drove downtown to the police station. They wanted to speak with the detectives in charge of her father's case. Kaydra wanted to see her father's remains and make arrangements to have his body cremated. Thereafter she could plan a celebration of his life. He was well known and very well-liked by so many on the Island. However, no one knew Johm as well as Alle and his ex-wife Natasha.

The receptionist told them that the detectives in charge of Ruiz's case were George Franken and Esmar Geil. However neither one of them were at the station. Alle asked for their cards so she could call them later that day.

"I would like to still view my father's remains," said Kaydra crying. "Who can I speak to about that who may be here?"

"The coroner is not available but you can call him if you wish. His name is Dr. Jan Fingal. Here is his card."

"I just want to see my father. Can't someone just take me to him?"

The receptionist could see how upset Kaydra was. "I'll call the Chief and tell him you're here. Please have a seat."

After 10 minutes, which seemed like an hour to Kaydra, Chief Biob Peterson appeared.

"Which one of you is the daughter of Johm Ruiz?"

"I am. My name is Kaydra Ruiz. This is my friend and my father's friend Alle Thiel."

"I am so sorry for your loss. I know how much your father was thought of. He was a good man. And Kaydra you have really become a beautiful lady. I remember you when you were much younger."

"Thanks Mr. Peterson, I remember you also. So when can I see him?"

"I'm sorry Kaydra, there is an ongoing investigation and there are some reports that the coroner is still waiting for. Until then, I can't let anyone but the investigators or the coroner into the morgue."

Kaydra let out a scream, got up from her chair and demanded to see her father. The Chief, Alle and the receptionist all came over to comfort Kaydra, but the Chief assured her that as soon as the final reports were complete on her father, he would contact her to make the necessary arrangements. That didn't seem to satisfy Kaydra, but Alle put her arm around Kaydra, thanked the Chief, and walked Kaydra back to her car.

"This is like a horrible nightmare. What am I supposed to do? Where am I going to stay? What do I do about my classes?"

"Kaydra you are welcome to stay at my home for as long as it takes to unravel this mystery. I'll call the detectives as soon as we get back to the house. Maybe they can shed some light on this tragedy."

Kaydra continued to cry and mutter all the way back to Alle's house. Nothing seemed to calm her. She fell asleep on Alle's couch thirty minutes after they arrived. Alle attempted to call the detectives but every message went to voice mail. Both women were confused and depressed. Alle was certain that the detectives would want to speak to them. Finally her phone rang. It was detective Franken. He told Alle that they were at the airport in the customs area speaking to Johm's co-workers. He assured her that he would make arrangements for Kaydra to view her father. Thereafter, Franken indicated that he had some questions he wanted to ask of them. He told them to come back to the police station the next day at 1:00 PM. Arrangements could then be made for viewing and questioning. Alle thanked the detective and told him that they would meet at that time.

It was 9:45 PM and Harrison and Bob were on their second drink at Ruth's Chris. Kelly was still not there.

"Kelly is never late. That is one of her pet peeves," said Bob. "For her to be this late and not call me is very unusual. Something is wrong."

Bob had been attempting to call her cell phone for 30 minutes but it kept going to voice mail. Harrison was also worried. He kept thinking about what happened on the beach that morning. Bob decided to go up to their room to look for her. First he stopped at the Tradeswind's restaurant to see if maybe she was there. But the receptionist told him that she hadn't seen her that evening. Bob went to their hotel room. The room door was ajar. There were several chairs turned over, several drink glasses broken and something that looked like blood was on the bed spread. Papers were thrown all over the room. The safe was open and empty.

That put Bob into a panic mode. He called Harrison and told him what he saw in his room. Harrison rushed to the room. Bob was sitting at the desk with his hands on his face.

"She's gone. Someone grabbed her," cried Bob.

"I'll call security," said Harrison. "There has to be some explanation. Did you and Kelly have some words before we were too meet? Are you sure she knew the time we were meeting tonight?"

"She made the reservations. She's gone. Someone took her. What in the Hell are we supposed to do now?"

CHAPTER 4

The Cedar-Riverside neighborhood in downtown Minneapolis was nicknamed "Little Mogadishu" because of its Somali American population. On Somali Street, a mall rested inside a wide, blue bungalow. There, different vendors in stalls sold traditional clothes, food items and bedclothes.

A few feet away, a two-story brick building housed the Masjid Darul-Quba Mosque and a cultural center. Opposite the mall, several mothers strolled with their children in a small park. Signs of Somali restaurants and other small businesses dotted other streets in the area.

Minnesota was home to over 70,000 Somali Americans. That was about 40% of all Somalis living in the entire United States. Some of them relocated in the aftermath of Somalia's civil war in 1991. It was a new environment for the refugees, but many of them faced the challenge of keeping their families away from violence, even in Minneapolis. 4,000 of the Somalis left Minneapolis to go to St. Cloud, Minnesota, about 60 miles north to escape the Minneapolis and "Little Mogadishu' bloodshed. The Somali community in St. Cloud faced its own darkest times when, in 2016, there was a mass stabbing spree at the Crossroads Center shopping mall. That assault was initiated by a discontent Somali refugee. After 10 people were critically injured, the St. Cloud police shot and killed the perpetrator. Violence and crime were everywhere the Somali people went.

Some of the viciousness was brought on by the Somali community itself. First, there was isolation with lack of assimilation of the Somali Muslim community wherever they lived. Second, the teaching of Sharia law in principally Muslim schools, in Minneapolis. Those were the two main reasons why the locals feared the growing number of Somali Muslim gangs. That lessened the attempt for assimilation and caused a huge crime problem in Minneapolis.

When Harrison Ramsey and Bob Walker were in under graduate school, their youthful progressive leanings lead them to believe that they could do something, even if it was a small gesture, to better assimilate the Somali community. They contacted several Christian agencies who viewed the arrival of Somali immigrants as an opportunity to serve and spread the Christian gospel. Neither Harrison nor Bob were religious people, but at least it was a place for them to start. Their efforts led them to an organization known as the Somali Adult Literacy Training or 'SALT'. Harrison and Bob, along with nearly 200 other volunteers, assisted refugees with English literacy lessons, conversational English and an understanding of the history of the United States to entice as many of the refugees, as possible to study for, and eventually pass, the US citizenship test. Bob even convinced Kelly to help. She was very enthusiastic. Unbeknownst to either Harrison or Bob at the time, bringing Kelly into the organization was a consequence that would change their lives. The older Somali men despised women teaching girls and especially teaching boys.

Harrison, Bob and Kelly spent many evenings, for several weeks, at the local cultural center in 'Little Mogadishu' assisting any refugees who wanted to assimilate and become citizens. Kelly seemed to naturally take to those tasks much better than either Harrison or Bob. Many evenings Kelly would go to the cultural center alone and meet her students. One evening when Kelly was tutoring a 16 year old girl, she suddenly felt a huge hand on her shoulder. When she looked around she saw a large Somali man, about 6 foot two inches tall and well over 200 pounds. He was not wearing the westernized jeans and t-shirt that most Somali men were becoming accustomed to. He had a traditional sarong-like garment which he wore around his waist with a large cloth wrapped around the upper part of his body. On his head was an embroidered turban which the Somali called a taqiyah. The expression on the man's face frightened Kelly.

"Can I help you sir?" said Kelly.

"Women are not allowed to teach girls in this cultural center. It a Mosque for prayers only, not a school. Please leave."

"Sir I come here often and…" the man interrupted her and grabbed Kelly's other shoulder with his other hand.

"Didn't you understand me?"

Now Kelly, who was alone that evening, was really scared. She got up, grabbed the girl by her hand and turned to go out the nearest door onto Riverside Drive. Just across the street from the Mosque was a local Starbucks. Cars were circling the parking lot outside the coffee shop searching for a rare open space. Inside what was commonly known as the 'Somali Starbucks', crowds of Somali men clustered together at tables, greeting one another with handshakes and hugs. They sipped coffee and tea, chatting in their native language. Their laughter and animated voices echoing off the walls. Someone looking for a lead on a job, or a good deal on a car or a legal or illegal way to make some money, dropped by that coffee house and asked around. This was now going to be the place Kelly would meet her students for their lessons. She was not happy. Maybe Harrison or Bob would have a better idea. However, Kelly was sure that she needed to mention what happened to her at the cultural center next time the "SALT' contingency got together.

The next day Kelly called Bob and told him about the incident at the cultural center.

"Do you know who it was that booted you out of the center?" asked Bob.

"No, but he was one scary and unhappy Somali."

I have told you several times that you shouldn't go to the Mosque by yourself. Either Harrison or I or another male 'SALT' member needs to accompany you. Otherwise you knew that this was going to happen at some time."

"Let's call a meeting of as many 'SALT' members we can in the next few days to discuss this issue. If we are trying to assimilate young people into American society, we need to have a plan and make sure all of us are safe in "Little Mogadishu".

Harrison and Bob lived together in an off campus apartment while they were in college and then stayed in the apartment while working on their Masters Degree. Bob then suggested, "There is a community hall in my apartment building. Harrison and I will email the 'SALT' group and get as many together as possible to try to achieve a plan."

Ten days after the email went out, a meeting was held in the apartment's community room. 31 'SALT' members attended. Half of them were women. Kelly recapped her frightening episode at the Mosque. One of the 'SALT' members, Marc Harper, immediately rose and said, "I know exactly who you are describing. His name is Diric Omar. He runs the financing and security for the Mosque and the cultural center. He needs to be handled gently. He is very powerful and well respected in the community. He raises a lot of money for the Somali community and the Mosque. When I say a lot of money, I mean a lot! No one is quite sure where all the money comes from and no one seems to want to ask. He has a small group of men who work under him. They are known around the community as his "muscle."

"What the Hell does that mean? Is he some kind of Godfather for the community?" asked another 'SALT' member.

"I have no idea," commented Marc. But maybe two or three men from our group can set a meeting with him and educate him about what we are attempting to do for his community. There must be some way to get his approval and be able to use the cultural center without being harassed. Even if we have to help him raise money. I'm sure he'll have rules, but if we want to continue our work we'll need to accommodate him. He literally runs 'Little Mogadishu'."

After a long discussion, it was determined that Harrison, Marc and Kelly would somehow arrange a meeting with him to discuss 'SALT's program. There was a lot of concern that it may be a bad idea to have a woman be part of that meeting. However, a large group of those attending that evening believed that it was imperative that this important member of the Somali community recognize woman as part of 'SALT's endeavor. Marc was the person who emphasized that to the group. Marc and Kelly seemed to get along well from the first time they met. They actually became very good friends. They began communicating about many things, not just 'SALT' over the phone.

Through Marc Harper's connections in the Somali community, a meeting was arranged with the three "SALT' members and Diric Omar. It was to be held at the Somali Starbucks at 11:00 AM. That was the slowest part of the day for the coffee house. All three members were glad the meeting was going to be held in a public place in the late morning hours. As a precaution, there was no mention of Kelly being part of the meeting.

At 11:00 AM the day of the meeting, Harrison, Marc and Kelly were sitting at a table for 4 waiting for Mr. Omar. Each had ordered a coffee. At 11:20 they started to get a little nervous and were afraid that Mr. Omar would be a no show. What would they do then? As they started to discuss their next move, Diric Omar entered the coffee house with two additional men. This time Omar was wearing blue jeans, a white T-shirt with white Nike running shoes. The three Somali men walked over to "SALT's table for 4 and all stared at Kelly.

"What is she doing here?" asked Omar.

"She a member of our organization and only one of many other woman in the organization who want to help your community. We are here to communicate to you our organizational mission and are looking for you and the members of your Mosque to help, or at least tolerate, our efforts to assimilate your community into the Minneapolis community. She is here in good faith and we mean no disrespect to you or to any member of your Mosque," uttered Marc very cautiously.

"As long as she is here with you I will listen to what you propose."

Marc then introduced himself, Harrison and Kelly to Omar. He gave him a very short resume of each of them including where they were going to school and for what purposes. Then there was a pause as Marc waited for Omar to introduce himself and the two men with him. No introductions were uttered. So after a short silence, Marc then suggested that they all find a table for 6.

As Omar sat at the empty fourth chair he said, "There is no need for that. These men will just go over to the door and wait for me. Your schooling and your families don't interest me. It is my responsibility only to secure the Mosque and cultural center and make certain that they are well funded. Now what is it that you thought was so important to speak with me? I only have a limited amount of time. My responsibilities keep me and my staff very busy. So, please, get on with what you want from me and my people."

Marc again took the lead. He was the one of the three most familiar with the community and had several Somali friends he socialized with. In a very quick and miniscule manner Marc explained to Omar the mission of 'SALT' and the manner it could be implemented within the Somali community for the purpose of assimilation of Omar's community into the Minneapolis community and his people's new homeland.

"So you believe that your community's way of life and laws are superior to our culture and Sharia laws?"

Kelly then quickly answered. "That is not our belief or purpose. Our organization does not want to change your community's culture. We don't believe in that. However, if any of the community wants to permanently reside in this Country, it is important that they understand and follow our laws."

Omar was agitated that a woman spoke to him in that tone. "So woman, if there were certain tactics that the Mosque may use for its funding that may not comply with your laws, what would you do?"

Kelly wanted to answer Omar's inquiry, but she was quickly hushed. "Let this Mr. Marc answer," insisted Omar.

"Mr. Omar we are not your enemy. We respect the rights of all people including woman. Kelly is her own person and has her own ideas and ambitions. We must all respect that. It is part of our culture. We want to respect your culture. Please let her speak. That is all part of our mission."

"Then I will let her speak as to my concerns."

Kelly was surprised how quickly Marc stood up for her. That to her was an endearing quality. She liked that. Marc had impressed her since they met the first time at a 'SALT' meeting. So she began to speak.

"Mr. Omar, we are teachers. Our organization is here to educate your community and to help assimilate only those, from your community, who want to be assimilated into our culture and laws. We are not here to extinguish your culture and we are not in the law enforcement business.

What you do to raise funds for your Mosque is your business. We would even help you raise funds if you may want us to help."

Diric Omar stared at Kelly with the same look that he gave her the first time they met. That was the same look he gave to Alle Thiel when he evicted her from his office building. However, Kelly's last comment stuck in Omar's mind. There was a long pause and then Omar got up from his chair. He looked at Marc and Harrison. Both were somewhat confused.

Then Omar said with a condition of authority, "So long as you do not interfere with my fund raising methods for the Mosque and cultural center your organization may be allowed to teach your laws and culture for the strict purposes of assimilation of only those who want to be assimilated into your community. But this can be done only under certain conditions.

First, there will be no teaching during the 5 daily prayers in the Mosque; second, your people will respect my peoples culture and dress; third, if any woman comes into the Mosque or culture center she must be accompanied by at least one man and she must wear a hijab; fourth, no matter what you see or hear in my community, you will not discuss it with anyone, especially your law enforcement people; and lastly, someday I may ask one, or even all of you individuals to do a favor for me and my community concerning fund raising. No matter what that favor may be you must agree to comply. Do you understand these conditions?"

All three were very confused about the last condition, but Kelly had offered their help. But, how could they agree to something that they had no idea what it was? They quietly discussed Omar's conditions for a few minutes. They concluded that whatever Omar may ask of them, they may very well not be able to even do. Also they knew that after they graduated they would probably no longer be continuing with 'SALT'. None of them even knew where they would end up after graduation. Omar would probably forget about the condition or they would be far away from 'Little Mogadishu'. So, after their few minutes of discussion they all agreed to comply with Omar's conditions. By agreeing to Omar's conditions that kept 'SALT's mission intact. With their oral agreement in place, Omar turned around and walked over to the two men he entered with and left the coffee house. None of the three had any idea how and why the ramifications of that Agreement would eventually change their lives.

During the 12 months after the agreement was initiated, the 'SALT' organization strictly followed Omar's agreed upon conditions. The members of 'SALT' who regularly met with individual Somalis or the Somali community as a whole, attempted to do everything in their playbook to attempt to assimilate the community into the Minneapolis community. In some 'SALT' member's minds it was like swimming upstream. Less than a couple dozen Somali residents agreed to try to assimilate and follow the local laws. Most of them were young adults who spoke excellent English and desired to have a higher education, to achieve the community's respect and receive a degree from an accredited college. Kelly tutored two Somali woman who eventually graduated from a 4 year college and went on to become gainfully employed by large fortune 500 companies. Both Harrison and Bob, along with many of their co-volunteers, felt their efforts and time were useless. Many of the 'SALT' members even quit working with Somali people and went on to work with other minorities in the city. It was a disappointing experience.

After Harrison and Bob graduated with their respective Master Degrees, Harrison was hired by Marriott Hotels. He left Minneapolis to go to Akron, Ohio, as an assistant food and beverage manager for a Courtyard Hotel. Bob was hired by IBM as the regional manager of sales for the Salt Lake City region. Bob and Kelly kept in constant contact during her last year at St. Thomas. They would visit each other from time to time. Kelly also kept in close touch with Marc Harper. The two of them became very close friends. They socialized frequently the year Bob was in Salt Lake City.

The year Kelly graduated Bob wanted her to apply for a position with IBM hoping that she would be able to get a job close to him. Kelly had a difficult decision to make. It was almost a foregone conclusion that Kelly and Bob would eventually marry. However, Kelly knew she had feelings for Marc. But she also had known Bob for a long time and there were feelings there also. Through much reasoning and contemplating by Kelly, she knew she had to make a decision. Everyone in her life, except Marc, knew she should marry Bob. Kelly and Marc met one evening where Kelly buried her heart to Marc. She didn't know what to do.

Marc was not as ambitious as Kelly and marriage wasn't on his mind at that time. He said that maybe in the future if she was willing to wait and they spent more time together, they could become a couple. Marc loved Kelly, but was not in the same league as Harrison, Bob or Kelly. He could hardly afford college. He came from a poor family and he spent a lot of time by himself. His father was hardly ever around. He worked two jobs while Marc was attending school.

So after much thought, Kelly seemed to come to her senses and decided to marry Bob. But her feelings for Marc would never change. So Bob and Kelly became engaged to be married. IBM agreed to hire Kelly as an assistant office manager for the Ogden, Utah office. So Bob and Kelly were fairly close to each other.

Over the next few years Harrison continued to get promoted and was transferred to several other cities as manager for more upscale Marriot properties. He met many women and nearly became engaged to one of them, but his career always came first. Until he was promoted to the top position in one of Marriot's finest hotels, he wasn't ready to settle down.

After years of working in different positions in various Marriot properties all over the country, Harrison finally received the news that he was going to become the overall manager of the Aruba Marriott Hotel & Casino. That was one of Marriot's premier properties. With its large casino it was one of the most profitable properties in Marriot's enterprise. Harrison finally felt that he had made it. Harrison was in his position at the Aruba Marriot for only a few weeks when, out of the blue, he received a surprising call from an old friend, Marc Harper.

Bob and Kelly got married 18 months after Kelly graduated. Both moved up the ladder at IBM but never worked in the same city. Finally, the two decided to move back to Minneapolis and live together instead of meeting on weekends. Also, in the back of Kelly's mind, Marc, who she still considered a good friend, was still in the Twin Cities. So both,

Bob and Kelly applied for positions anywhere in the Twin Cities area. Bob got hired by 3M Company in St. Paul as the assistant manager of the consumer goods division for the company. It was a high paying, highly visible job. Kelly was hired by SuperValu in Eden Prairie, Minnesota. She was the assistant manager of the Human Resource division. Another high paying, highly visible job. They both felt very lucky. They purchased a large 3 bedroom home on Bohland Avenue in the high end area of Highland Park in St. Paul. Harrison was a little jealous. He was still single and 4000 miles away from his best friends. Once Harrison knew that Bob and Kelly where fully settled and back in Minnesota, they received a call from Harrison concerning his phone call from Marc Harper.

Marc Harper had graduated from Hamline University in St. Paul, Minnesota, with his B.S. degree in secondary education. His emphasis was on mathematics. He got a small scholarship and payed for the rest of his education by taking out student loans. He graduated several years before Bob and Harrison. He was a school teacher at Cretin Derham Hall, a private Catholic High School in St. Paul, teaching 12th grade trigonometry as well as other math classes for freshman and sophomore students. He was also the junior varsity football coach. The money was not great and the hours were even worse. He kept in touch with several people from the Somali community with whom he became good friends. He had heard that Bob and Kelly had moved back to Minnesota. He wondered if he should call them to get together for old time sake. That was when he received a call from Diric Omar.

CHAPTER 5

Marc was sitting at his desk in his class room. His last trigonometry class of the day had just ended. He was preparing for football practice when his cell phone rang. He didn't recognize the number on the phone. Usually a name would come up, unless it wasn't in his contacts. But, he answered it anyway.

"Mr. Omar, what a surprise. It's been a long time since we spoke to each other. Maybe 4 or 5 years. How are you?" said an astonished Marc Harper.

"Actually it's been almost 6 years. Thank you for asking about me, I am just fine." His attitude on the phone was much different than when they met at the Somali Starbucks years ago.

"Is there something I can do for you?"

"That is why I have called. I have had my people tracking you and your two friends since our meeting at Starbucks those many years ago. I understand that your friend Harrison Ramsey is now in charge of the second largest Hotel in Aruba. Also, that woman I met has married your friend Bob Walker. Both now have very good employment here in the Twin Cities. I have kept track of their many relocations and employments these last 7 years. And I understand that you and Kelly have become really good friends. I am a fair man and will not utter a word about that to anyone."

Marc was shocked at what Omar was inferring about Kelly and him. But he ignored the comment

Omar continued, "Now you and your friends are finally located perfectly for my fund raising business needs. That is why I am calling. At our meeting, years ago, you appeared to be the person in charge for your organization."

Marc was overwhelmed and quite confused. Why would Diric Omar care about their lives and who was in charge of a small committee at 'SALT'? As far as Marc could recall, the 'SALT' personnel had always followed all of his requirements when they met with the Somali community. Marc and his friends never saw Omar again after that meeting in Starbucks years ago. It has been over 5 years since Marc resigned from 'SALT'. He had kept in touch with several men who use to live in "Little Mogadishu" and they had even became friends. He frequently got together to socially with them. But that was the only connection he had left with the Somali community, even though his friends moved out of that community several years ago.

"You remember our oral agreement that day we met don't you?"

"It's been a long time, Mr. Omar, but I am certain that 'SALT' followed all of your demands. I cannot vouch for anyone in the organization after Harrison, Kelly or I resigned from 'SALT'. Is someone now violating your requirements?"

"No, be at ease, nothing like that. 'SALT' is long gone. However, I will give your organization high marks for attempting to assimilate my community into the culture and laws of Minneapolis. However, I believed that from the first time we met I knew that the middle and upper class American youth associated with your organization would never be able to connect to the people in my community. Only a handful of my people left my community for your American dream. Where they are now does not interest me."

Marc's mind was wandering wildly trying to understand what it was that Omar was calling about. Was it because of his friendship with several Somali men?

"I understand that you and several young men from my community have become friends. I applaud you for that. You even went to several Minnesota Viking football games together. They were a little confused about the rules. I never understood why you Americans call that game football. All they do is run and pass that funny shaped ball. Football is a game Somali people play. You call my game soccer. When did you Americans steal that name for your stupid game? But I digress."

As Omar was rambling, Marc then remembered one of his requirements that day at Starbucks. What kind of favor did Omar want from him? It's been years since he spoke with him, or even visited 'Little Mogadishu'. Given the problems of crime, intimidation and the lack of assimilation between the Somali community and the residents of the Twin Cities and St. Cloud over the last few years, Marc began to get quite apprehensive.

"Mr. Harper, or may I call you Marc? You remember agreeing to do me a favor someday concerning my fund raising activities, when I asked you, don't you?"

"I believe so, but that was so long ago."

"Time is a difficult concept for Americans to understand. Muslims concepts of time are enduring. Don't you think so Marc?"

Marc had no idea what he meant by that or what to even say. There was a long pause. Marc knew he should answer Omar, but he really didn't want to commit to anything. Seven years was a long time to keep a promise to do someone some little unknown favor.

"Marc, let me put it to you in this way. Your small committee that met with me years ago asked for my permission to try to assimilate my people to your traditions, culture and laws. With no argument and my blessing I agreed to your request. It had nothing to do with me that your organization failed. Your people were young and naïve. I don't hold that against you or your organization. However, in my culture a deal is a deal. So this favor I am asking for is really a favor that will benefit both of us. I know about your job teaching at that religious school and coaching those young boys that game you call football. I also know you don't make any real money for all the hours you work. That must be tough on your wife and kids. This favor would be an opportunity for you to keep that thankless job and also work for me to do fund raising and make some additional money. Think about what you could do if you made more money than you ever dreamed you could at your current employment.

You and your wife, or maybe you and Kelly, would be able to travel and buy some nice luxuries."

Marc had no idea what Omar was talking about. He also took offense to the comment about Kelly. What kind of fund raising work would Marc do for Omar, yet keep his current employment and still make some extra money? It had to be illegal or immoral, at least under American laws. Marc could never agree to that.

"Okay. I'm listening," said Marc cautiously.

"Before I discuss my favor any further, you have to agree to convince Mr. Ramsey and your friend Kelly to all be part of what I am going to ask of you."

"I can't agree to that Mr. Omar. I speak with them from time to time, but I can't agree to something that I have no control over. After all, I hardly even see them anymore," lied Marc.

Omar's tone quickly changed and Marc knew it right away. Marc became frightened. He didn't know what was about to come.

"I am speaking about a lot of money. You and your friends will benefit from some of that money by undertaking very little tasks. I and my security task force will maintain the largest risks. There will be some risks that you and your friends will have to take. But, I am certain you can convince your friends to cooperate. My culture and laws has its ways of convincing people. So I am certain that you and your friends will agree to become a part of my organization. So let's now understand that this favor has become a demand. Do you comprehend what I am saying?"

Marc was aware of what happens, in the Somali community, when anyone angers one of their leaders. There were several leaders who had organizations. Each ran a part of the Somali community. Omar was one of those leaders. If someone angered a leader, all of a sudden that person or persons ended up with debilitating injuries, or even worse, or were never seen again. Could dissenting to become a part of Omar's organization bring such a harsh outcome on him and his friends? Omar than went on to explain to Marc exactly what this favor would entail.

Marc could not believe that this was actually happening to him. Without any time to think, he had to make a decision. Marc knew that Omar was not going to let him take any time to discuss this demand with his old friends. So Marc begrudgingly agreed to Omar's demand. In the back of his mind he was so upset that he had ever agreed to that stupid demand years ago. Never in his wildest dreams did he contemplate that something like this would constitute 'a favor'.

Once Marc agreed, Omar went into the specifics of exactly what his favor entailed for Marc and his friends. After listening for about a half an hour, he wondered how he would ever approach his friends to become part of Omar's very illegal organization. His future life and livelihood depended on complying. He thought that he would speak with Kelly first. They understood each other well and their relationship would make the discussion easier. He knew Harrison wouldn't initially agree but Marc knew that he had Kelly's ear and she would understand the predicament much better than Harrison. After all, this could be a life or death decision for all of them. Omar's tentacles were very long. With that in mind, the money promised to Marc and his friends would be the catalyst that would help him and Kelly convince Harrison. Marc's dilemma was how Kelly would explain this to Bob. Omar didn't even mention Bob's name. He would call Kelly and arrange to meet and discuss Omar's 'favor' and the consequences for declining. What a mess over an insignificant conditional agreement that happened years ago.

What has happened to Kelly? Bob was frantic and Harrison was shocked. Harrison instructed his hotel security detail to search the entire hotel facilities and the casino. But, Kelly was nowhere to be found.

Has anyone touched anything in the hotel room?" asked Harrison to the head of his security and to Bob.

Both said no.

"Then I will call the police and ask them to bring in a CSI unit."

Harrison then called the police who indicated that it was now 11:45 PM and the woman had only been missing since 9:00 PM. It was less than 24 hours. So the police asked Harrison to continue to do his due diligence in attempting to find her. If there was no luck by the next evening, her husband could come to the police station and file a missing person incident report. The police asked Harrison to put the husband up in a different room for the night and to cordon off the room and not allow anyone, especially the cleaning crew or the husband, into the room.

"Don't you understand what the Walker's room looks like?" pleaded Harrison to the police. "Someone abducted a hotel guest from my hotel. I need you to send investigators to the hotel immediately. This Island depends on tourism. You remember Natalee Holloway, right?"

"That ship has sailed Mr. Ramsey. You are aware of the procedure for missing persons. You have a very competent security force. Have Ms. Walker's husband call us tomorrow late afternoon if Ms. Walker is not found by then."

Harrison was furious with the police and the whole situation they were involved with. Bob confronted Harrison and asked him if Kelly's disappearance could have anything to do with the incident on the beach earlier that afternoon with that John Smith guy. Bob thought Harrison told him that they would discontinue the scheme until the death of Johm Ruiz was solved. Harrison remembered that conversation but was very confused. He had heard of the name John Smith, but he thought Bob had been told his real name. The man on the beach was a member of Omar's organization. His name was Brad Nickolas. Harrison wanted to know if Kelly had explained to Bob that the scheme couldn't be just called off. The risk of stopping midstream on any transfers of funds would cause a ripple effect back to 'Little Mogadishu' and no one wanted that. Bob looked very confused.

"Kelly just told me she would tell me later that evening what was going on. I thought that John Smith was going to hurt Kelly. And you told me you would hold up on the scheme until everything was fixed," said Bob who was now getting even more confused.

"Bob what is it that you think is happening?" asked Harrison. "What has Kelly told you about the operation?"

"Not much. I just assumed that you were skimming some small sums of money from the casino and we were to each get a cut if we found some private banks around the Caribbean, during our travels, to launder the money until it was safe for all three of us to split it. Half to you and half to us."

"That's not what Kelly told you? Was it?"

"Well she really didn't explain everything so I just assumed." "Have you spoken with Marc Harper?"

"Marc Harper? That's a name from our past. I haven't spoken with him for years. He does live somewhere in St. Paul where Kelly and I live, but I have only seen him a couple of time in the last 6 or 7 years. What does he have to do with this?"

"Oh my God! Kelly really hasn't told you about our call from Marc Harper. You really don't know what we have gotten ourselves involved in, do you?"

"I have no idea what you're talking about, but if you and Marc Harper are the reason someone grabbed Kelly I will never forgive you."

"Bob, I had no idea that Kelly didn't tell you about our operation with Marc. I knew she wasn't going to tell you the full story since we were still getting further instructions from Marc. But most important she wanted you to have plausible deniability if things went wrong."

"You are confusing me and really scaring me. God Damit Harrison we have been friends forever. Since when did you and Kelly make some kind of pack to keep me out of anything happening with the two of you?"

Harrison then reminded Bob about the meeting with Diric Omar at the Starbucks over 7 years ago. Bob was not part of the committee that met with Omar. Harrison reiterated that Omar was a very scary person. He reminded Bob about the terms set up by Omar for the 'SALT' organization to continue to help educate and assimilate the Somali community into the culture of Minneapolis.

Bob's memory had to be refreshed. Harrison reminded him of one of the requirements that the three committee members had to agree to. It was a favor for Omar at some time in the future. Harrison confessed to Bob that Marc had been contacted by Omar several months ago and threatened the committee, including Bob since he had married Kelly. If the three of them didn't help Omar with his current fund raising operation in Minneapolis, all of their lives may be in danger. The favor was actually a demand and Omar had a long reach. The committee just didn't understand 'Little Mogadishu's' way of life at the time.

"So what you are telling me is that this 'operation' you are involved in is being run by the Somali mob out of 'Little Mogadishu" and we have no choice but to comply or be subject to bodily harm or maybe even death!"

"I'm afraid so. The only upside is we are going to make some money. Maybe not a large amount of money but enough to live a little better life," admitted Harrison.

"You make this sound like it is a good thing. Are you crazy? Why in the world would Marc, you and Kelly agree to this crazy scheme?"

"Let's not go into that right now. We are where we are. Kelly is missing because you interfered with a transfer of a lot of money this morning. We need to make this right," Harrison confessed. "If Kelly doesn't show up tonight, I'll call the police tomorrow and make this sound like an abduction and not reveal any of the underlying facts. But we need to contact Marc. He may be able to talk to his contacts to find out what happened to Kelly and when she will be returned."

At that point Bob called Harrison a Son of a Bitch and took a hard swing at him. Harrison ducked and jumped on Bob and held him down.

"I get your frustration old friend. But let's stick to our immediate problem, your wife. Okay? If I let you go, will you be reasonable and start to fit into, and accept the program?"

Bob begrudgingly nodded yes, but was as furious as he has ever been. He got up and restrained himself from swinging again. Harrison took him to an empty hotel room where he would stay until the authorities could scan their current room for fingerprints and DNA. Harrison told Bob to be cool about cooperating with the local authorities so as not to connect Kelly's disappearance with Johm Ruiz's death. Bob just shook his head. What have these people gotten him into? All because a bunch of young, naive students tried to help the Somali community assimilate into American culture. Now his wife was missing and maybe even dead. What a dilemma.

Harrison was aware, from his discussions with Marc, that Omar never told every person involved who all of the other people involved may be. That was Omar's way of making sure that if a part of the scheme was detected by authorities, the rest of the scheme could still move forward. Harrison intentionally left that fact out of his discussion with Bob. So

Bob went to his temporary room thinking the worse. He was extremely mad at Harrison and even Kelly. That was when he remembered several times that Kelly left their home and told Bob that she was meeting friends from her job for drinks or dinner. Was she really meeting Marc? Was there something going on between Marc and Kelly? Did Kelly leave to meet Marc? His mind could not stop speculating.

CHAPTER 6

The morning after Dr. Fingal was escorted out of the casino, he immediately went into his home office and finalized a fake toxicology report on Johm Ruiz. Dr. Fingal never sent any of the blood or tissue samples he obtained from Ruiz's autopsy to the Curacao lab. They were all still in the cooler at the police morgue. His reputation as a doctor, including his volunteer work, as the Island's coroner, didn't raise any red flags with the police, or anyone else. No one on the Island would believe that the doctor would do anything like that. The fake toxicology report didn't show anything criminal causing Johm Ruiz's death. Fingal indicated that Ruiz had an aneurysm in his brain. This abnormal bulge in the wall of his blood vessel in his brain could have ruptured at any time. No one could have known it had existed. An aneurysm has no symptoms. With that bogus toxicology report, Dr. Fingal wrote his final autopsy report indicating death by natural causes. That was what appeared on Ruiz's death certificate. Now Fingal's mind was focused exclusively on the fact that he no longer owed the Marriott Hotel casino any money. His debt would be extinguished. Fingal's wife was unaware of the Marriott casino's debt since it was only a debt on the books of the hotel. No money was ever taken out of any of Fingal's accounts to pay any of that debt. He still owed several thousand dollars to the Hyatt Hotel Casino, but that he could pay off over a few weeks. An obsessive gamblers mind doesn't think of reality or consider the illegality of what they were doing. Now, he believed, he would still be able to keep his gambling obsession from his family and friends. At the time Fingal wrote his report, he didn't know about Kelly's disappearance.

He also had no idea about the scheme that was happening with Harrison. He was just an obsessive gambler in the wrong place at the wrong time.

The fake toxicology report was the perfect circumstance for Harrison to recruit Fingal to facilitate the scheme without letting the doctor understand the ramifications. Harrison, himself, had no idea if Ruiz was murdered or if he died a natural death. He just wanted to cover his ass and cover the people he knew he was working with, just in case there was wrong doing with Ruiz's death. Fingal would have done anything to have his gambling debt extinguished without any question as to why. Harrison knew that. After some sobering thoughts, he began to wonder why Harrison wanted him to do that favor for him. Maybe it could be used to his advantage in the future. Once a gambler, always a gambler. The only unknown was if Fingal could continue to have Harrison cover for him if he had future losses. But most gamblers always think that they're not going to lose. Fingal kept that thought in the back of his mind.

The next day Dr. Fingal took his report to the Chief of Police to show him the report. That was not the the normal course of action in these types of cases. Usually the Chief would keep a copy of the report. However, the Chief had full confidence that his coroner would file the original in the coroners' office.

"Biob, here is my final report on Ruiz's death. He died of natural causes. A non-diagnosed aneurysm burst and caused his immediate death."

"What about the toxicology report? Anything unusual in it?"

"It provided no evidence of any questionable substances in either his blood or tissues."

"What a tragedy. Johm was a wonderful and kind man. I'll contact his next of kin. Then I'll contact my detectives who will be overwhelmingly delighted."

Then Fingal took the original fake report and went into the morgue and took all of the blood and tissue samples and left the building.

Just before Chief Peterson started to call his detectives, his assistant informed him that Harrison Ramsey from the Marriott Hotel was on the phone and needed to speak with him immediately. The Chief acquiesced. He was informed, by Harrison, of the circumstances of one of the Marriott's guests missing including the disarray of her room. Harrison informed the Chief that he had requested police assistance along with the Marriott's security personnel to help locate Kelly Walker. For an Island that had such a low crime rate this shocked the Chief. And this came just after he had finished with Johm Ruiz's death case. He agreed to immediately send his detectives and the Island's CSI to the Marriott Hotel to work on Kelly's disappearance. However the Chief required that his detectives take the lead on the investigation. Harrison was not pleased with that decision but he didn't want to argue.

The Chief then called Alle Theil's home to speak with Kaydra Ruiz. He informed her that the autopsy and toxicology test were complete and that the results indicated that there had been no foul play in her father's death. It was strictly natural causes. She would now be able to go back to her home since it would no longer be considered a crime scene. The news that there was no crime involved was wonderful, however, her father was, none the less, dead. That didn't comfort her much.

"What kind of natural causes? Did the coroner elaborate?"

"Dr. Fingal indicated that your father died of a non-diagnosed aneurysm. It could have been there for years. Even since your father's birth."

"So what do I do now Chief?"

"I know the funeral director at the Olive Tree Funeral Home. I can call him now and have them pick up your father. You can meet him at the funeral home and make arrangements. I know a lot of people who would like to attend whatever service you decide."

"That funeral home is in San Nicholas," replied Kaydra. "That is the most southern city on the Island. A long way for me to go Chief."

"Kaydra, it's the location of the only crematorium on the Island. I knew your father well. He wanted to be cremated. And you know that no place is a long way on this small Island. But there are six Mausoleums on the Island. You can choose the one you want to entomb his remains. The director will take good care of your father. I'll make sure of that."

"I had no idea he wanted to be cremated. I really would like to bury him so I would have a location to go to speak with him."

"No one thinks that they would die so young, Kaydra. That's probably why he never mentioned it to you."

"But what if I want to bury him?

"Kaydra, there are strict laws concerning burial on this Island. Your father would've had to apply for a burial permit and paid for the plot before he passed in order to be buried."

"I understand. I think I knew about that but never really thought much about it. I really appreciate what you're doing Chief. I'll go to the funeral home first thing tomorrow. Again, I really appreciate your help."

"We all liked your father. I'm so sorry for your loss."

Kaydra hung up the phone and turned to Alle. She told Alle the entire conversation with Chief Peterson.

"I knew that Johm wanted to be cremated. We spoke about it several times. Don't worry, I'll be with you the entire time."

"My father was a lucky man. You're a good friend Alle. I would really like to go home tonight. I want to sleep in my own bed. Will you stay with me tonight?"

"Of course, my dear. We have a long day tomorrow."

Kaydra embraced Alle and thanked her for everything. Then she cried for a long time. Alle was sympathetic but she was surprised when she heard about the coroner's report. In her mind, she knew something else really happened to him. Why the coroner would come to the conclusion he did was somewhat of a mystery to Alle. She needed to ponder what was really happening. Was there going to be some kind of a sting at the mortuary? Was Omar involved with the coroner? Unfortunately, she also was not fully briefed on everything happening with the scheme, or, who else may be involved. Yet she knew that the report was a relief to Kaydra.

After Chief Peterson hung up with Kaydra, he called detective Franken.

"George, I have some good news and some bad news."

Franken and his partner were at the airport interviewing Coy Dirksz, Ruiz's boss.

"We're just finishing our interview with Coy, can I call you right back Chief?"

"You don't need to finish the interview with Coy. That's the good news. I just received information from Dr. Fingal that Ruiz died of a brain aneurism. It was natural causes. No crime there. You and Geil can close your file."

"Holy shit! That's good news."

"What the Hell does that mean?" the Chief said offensively.

"Oh Chief, I didn't mean it was good news that Johm died. I just meant..." "I guess I know what you meant George. Now do you want to know the bad news?"

"Lay it on me Chief. I'm just glad that the Ruiz case is over."

"Harrison Ramsey, the manager at the Marriott Hotel & Casino just called and told me that one of the hotel's frequent flyer guests has disappeared."

"What do you mean disappeared?"

"Kelly Walker. Her husband, Bob, and Harrison Ramsey are good friends. Bob and Kelly Walker stay at the hotel six to seven times a year. From what Harrison told me, her room was really a mess. Chairs turned over. The bedspread a mess. The contents of the desk were all over the floor. The safe was opened and it was empty. It was not forcibly opened. Whoever opened it had to know the code. Someone may have abducted her. She must have put up a fight. I have already notified CSI and they are on their way to the hotel to do their thing. Some substance that looked like it may be blood was visible, but CSI will check that out. You and Geil need to get to the Marriot first thing in the morning. Find out what CSI discovered. Canvass the whole top floor and take statements from all the Tradewind's guests. Talk to other residents in the hotel and the staff. Someone must have seen something. Interview the husband, but be discrete. He claims he was with Ramsey at Ruth's Chris waiting to meet Ms. Walker for dinner. She never showed so they went up to her room. That's when they saw its condition. Ms. Walker was nowhere to be found. Ramsey had his hotel security rummage the entire hotel. She is missing. I hope she just snuck out for a drink or took a walk on the beach. She may even show up tonight, but I don't think so." All Franken could think about was whether or not this was another Natalee Holloway! But he didn't say it.

"OK Chief, we're on it."

The next morning both detectives arrived at the Marriott Hotel at 7:30. On the way to the hotel detective Geil called CSI to ascertain what they found. There was no blood. It was some other substance that looked like blood. The only fingerprints found were Bob and Kelly Walkers. Even the maintenance staff wore gloves when they cleaned the rooms. So they had no idea who had been in that room. But what was found was Kelly's cell phone, wallet with nothing missing, her passport and her keys. It looks like she had been abducted, but CSI had no answers.

Bob was fatigued. He couldn't sleep at all in his temporary room. All he thought about was what could be happening to Kelly? And he wondered if there was something going on between Kelly and Marc. Did she leave to meet him? During the night, he finally decided to leave the room and spent hours walking the Palm Beach area including most of the commercial areas in the high rise district that he and Kelly regularly frequented. He found nothing. And no one had seen her.

Harrison and his security staff went through all camera footage on the floor near Kelly's room and all exits. What they saw was bewildering. At 8:45 PM, just before Kelly was to meet Harrison and Bob at the restaurant, Kelly came out of the room carrying a large black leather bag. She took the elevator to the first floor. She exited the hotel through the revolving door from the casino to the parking lot adjacent to the hotel. She turned south and walked past the two large Marriott timeshare buildings and disappeared as she turned toward the beach. She was alone and didn't look injured. She did look like she was on a mission. Why would she do that? She left her phone, wallet, passport and keys. Very strange. It looked as if what she was doing had some sort of purpose.

Harrison showed the detectives and Bob the camera footage. Everyone was confused. Neither Harrison nor Bob knew why she would have done that. Where was she going? Harrison knew there was over half a million dollars in their hotel room. Bob thought it was just a couple of thousand in the safe, but neither said anything. CSI didn't find any money except for a couple of hundred dollars in Kelly's wallet. Neither Bob nor Harrison mentioned the money to the detectives. Bob still wondered if Kelly was meeting Marc. But again he said nothing.

"Okay gentleman, what the Hell is going on?" asked Franken. "One of you must know something."

Bob looked relieved that Kelly was still alive and well. But he had no idea why Kelly would disappear with such a small amount of money, especially in the manner she did. Harrison had more serious thoughts. He knew Kelly had to have some motive to be taking all of that money and run. After all, that wasn't their money. It belonged to either Diric Omar or his right hand man, Brad Nickolas. All of them now could be in serious danger.

Bob was holding back tears of joy while Harrison needed to make sure the detectives would leave the situation in the hands of the hotel's security detail. The last thing Harrison wanted was the Aruba police investigating them.

"Detectives, now that we know Ms. Walker is alive and well, why don't you leave my security contingency to handle the issue. Bob and Kelly are my good friends. We can find her and we can handle all issues internally. There has to be a logical explanation as to why Kelly did this. After all, I have known her for years. More than likely Kelly will show up sometime today. If my security people don't figure this out, I'll give you a call. Actually, I'll give you a call even if this turns out just to be a prank."

Both of the detectives really thought that would be a good idea. It was so seldom that they investigated missing persons on the Island. However, Franken, the more experienced detective knew that his boss would never allow that.

"Mr. Ramsey, I'm sure my boss would require us to stay on this case until Kelly either returns or is found and everything is fully explained. We have already spent time and money on our CSI people. If you want to call Chief Peterson, feel free to do that. Otherwise we will stick around and continue our investigation."

"Fine, but keep me updated," reluctantly said Harrison. "I will continue to have my security people look for Kelly."

Franken had no problem with that and expressed that to Harrison. Thereafter, Franken obtained a picture of Kelly from Bob and he took her passport that had her picture. Both detectives then left the hotel and started to trace Kelly's steps to attempt to try to find out where she may have fled and why.

Bob immediately turned to Harrison and said, "Where in the Hell would Kelly go and why would she just take a few thousand dollars. That was all that must have been in the safe. Do you know what's going on? Is Marc Harper on the Island somewhere? Does it have something to do with the episode concerning John Smith on the beach yesterday? That scared her and me. Maybe there's more money involved? No one seems to tell me anything about this scheme. I thought this was just a simple scheme to skim some casino funds for the three of us to divide. Now it looks as if you and Kelly have much more going on."

"Your right Bob. The dinner last night was for the purpose of telling you everything. I'm sorry about leaving you out of the loop on the true scheme. But Kelly really didn't want you to have to get involved. And no Marc Harper is not on the Island. As far as I know he has never visited Aruba. Why would you ask that?"

"I thought we were best friends. We never kept secrets from each other. Now I am really pissed. If anything happens to Kelly, that's on you. And who really is John Smith? Does he or doesn't he work for you?"

"Come with me and I will explain everything to you."

"Not now. I need to find Kelly. She owes me an explanation first. For all I know she is either running with the money or hiding it somewhere or running away with Marc. Either one is going to be a big problem for you. I have to find her before the detectives. For all I know, if they find her first with those funds, she'll be brought in and interrogated. I'm sure neither of us want that."

Harrison was somewhat embarrassed about the state of affairs with his best friend. He knew he needed to call Marc Harper in St. Paul and let him know what just happened and that Bob had some stupid idea that Marc and Kelly have something going on. After all Marc is married and has kids. He shivered thinking about the consequences of that call. There was more than a half million dollars missing along with Kelly Walker. How and why did this happen? How was Harrison going to explain it? Not only to Marc, but more importantly, to Brad Nickolas.

CHAPTER 7

It was 9:00 AM Saturday morning in St. Paul. Marc Harper was getting ready to leave his home for the junior varsity football game against St. Paul Central. Cretin Derham Hall was 4 and 0 for the season. Central was 1 and 3. Marc was optimistic about the game. He had several very impressive sophomore prospects. The varsity head coach had recently spoken to Marc about assigning several of Marc's better players to the varsity team. Several varsity players had suffered injuries. Marc liked to win and knew losing several of his best players would substantially hurt the team's future record. However, Marc understood how the system worked. Every junior varsity player was anxious for that invitation to move up to varsity, even if was just temporarily.

With his playbook in hand as he was stepping into his car, his cell phone rang. Marc didn't recognize the phone number. He thought it may be a robo call, but the area code was Aruba. So he answered the call. It was Harrison Ramsey. There were no pleasantries. Harrison came right to the point.

"Marc, we have a problem."

Harrison who's phone are you on?"

"I'm on a burner phone. I purchased several in case sensitive issues came up."

"Harrison I am on my way to my schools football game. You know I am the head coach. Can't this wait? Omar hasn't given me any funds in the last week. I have nothing to give Kelly. Let me call you later this afternoon."

"Marc, Kelly is missing. Worse than that, so is over a half million dollars."

"I don't understand. Let me get in my car. I'll put you on speaker. I need to get to this game."

"Screw the game. You won't be able to coach any sport if you have two broken knee caps."

"OK, slow down what in the Hell is happening?"

Harrison proceeded to explain the last several days to Marc starting with the death of Johm Ruiz through the hotel tape of Kelly fleeing with over half million dollars.

Marc's first question was, "Who in the Hell is Johm Ruiz?

"He's a customs supervisor for the Aruba airport. He works with someone we don't know. I'm sure Omar must have set him up as his connection in customs."

"Oh. I seem to remember a John Ruiz. I think I had dinner with him several years ago. He was a custom agent in Aruba then. He, Dr. Burton Woodcock and some other people, I can't remember who, had dinner at some expensive restaurant in Minneapolis. I can't remember all the details. Maybe it had something to do with our 'SALT days. Did this guy, Ruiz, overhear something? Do you know who may have killed him? Has anyone told Brad Nickolas about Ruiz's murder or the missing money? How about Omar. Does he know? And Kelly! Why would she disappear?"

"Slow down. No one knows about Omar's connection in customs. If someone in customs had anything to do with Ruiz's death he certainly didn't have my authority. Murder is not part of this scheme. As to Ruiz's murder I have handled that matter, just in case one of Omar's connections, or someone else, did have something to do with the murder. To tell you the truth, I don't really know if he was murdered. Nor do I even know if he is part of Omar's scheme. I just assumed he was, so I took care of the problem. I just hope it doesn't cost me my job. But the good news is now the police believe he died of natural causes. Kelly and the money, however, are a mystery. Has she contacted you?"

"This is the first I've heard of any of this. And why are you calling me? I had no idea that murder had any part of the scheme. Isn't this your problem? Everyone has their mission in this scheme. I have nothing to do with what may happen in Aruba or any of the other Caribbean Islands. It's your task to handle this Ruiz matter. Whatever you did to handle the cause of death, good for you. However, how could you not know whether or not he was actually murdered? Was there an autopsy?"

"Listen asshole. Don't put all this on my shoulders. This is on all of us. We need to find out about Ruiz's death. It may or may not have been a murder. My job may be in jeopardy even if he wasn't murdered. I hope I made the right decision. I just assumed Omar or someone else involved in the scheme had something to do with Ruiz's death. I thought that Irving may have overheard something between Johm and Kelly while coming through customs. I assumed that Irving may have threatened Johm that he would go to the police. But I can't confirm that. Maybe Irving is involved in the scheme. Right now I am more confused about what is actually happening and who is really involved. That is why I need your help. This has all become one big mess. You are the main contact with Omar. I am hoping that you can, in some subtle manner, find out who is really involved and what the Hell is going on with Kelly."

There was a pause with Marc saying nothing. So Harrison continued. "Now, about the money. It needs to be divided in half with each half deposited in two off shore banks by tomorrow afternoon. If it isn't you will be receiving a call from Omar. You got us into this scheme. You need to call your contacts today and find out if anyone in "Little Mogadishu" ordered a hit on Ruiz, or know the whereabouts of Kelly. We need to know her intentions. That is imperative. It may determine our futures. I have worked too hard to have my career end over this stupid scheme. And I will not spend time in any Federal prison. So either help us all out of this mess or go play your fucking football game. This is serious. Your choice."

Then Harrison hangs up.

While Marc and Harrison were discussing their recent issues, the first of five daily prayers for the Somali congregation was in progress. Omar was carefully, without being noticed, entering the back room at the Masjid Darul-Quba Mosque. The room was large enough to handle a small banquet. There were twelve oblong tables and several safes. Each table had two chairs and two money counting machines. Three of the tables were occupied by Somali girls, all under the age of 15, with their heads covered with the traditional hijab. Somali girls, under the age of 16, were not required to wear head coverings, but it was an important issue for Omar to have the girls be recognized as adult Muslims with the hope of instilling in them a sense of Muslim identity. Somalis living in Minneapolis were living within a larger society that didn't share the Muslim customs or laws. Omar shunned that.

Each of the girls where operating one of the money counter machines and were piling small and large bills in thousand dollar stacks. Omar slowly walked the room stroking each little girl's heads as he passed by them. He gave each girl a smile making sure they knew they were appreciated. Each girl's parent had no idea what was happening in that back room. They believed their daughters were attending religious school. The girls knew never to divulge what they were doing to anyone outside that room, especially their parents. They all craved for Omar's affection. They were well aware of the consequences of speaking to anyone about what went on at the culture center next to the Mosque.

Omar, as the finance minister for the Mosque, procured money not only for the Mosque but for other cultural events held in "Little Mogadishu". However the majority of money secured by Omar went to Omar and his 'security team'. Smaller amounts went to Harrison, Marc, Kelly, Alle, Brad and Irving. Omar had a militia of young Somali men involved in gambling, loan sharking and illicit business security. All local non-Somali owned small businesses were required to pay Omar a portion of their profits for security from being robbed or having their businesses being damaged by several rival Somali gangs. If any business refused or were short on their payments, his security detail would threaten bodily harm to the owner or a member of their family. The damage that may occur was dependent on how much was owed or the owner's lack of cooperating with paying their security payments. However, Omar's loyalty to his religion would never let his security team murder anyone. Omar never worried about any Minneapolis police interference with his businesses. After George Floyd's death, most of the Minneapolis police funding was reallocated. The police force became smaller and ineffective.

So the Minneapolis authorities never cared about what was happening in or around "Little Mogadishu". What was happening in Minneapolis gave Omar carte blanche to continue his collections for all of his business and fund raising. At least that was the impression Omar gave the 'SALT' committee members and others who owed him a favor.

As Omar was viewing his young girls putting together the spoils of his latest weeks financing, his cell phone buzzed. Because prayers were going on he had turned off his phone. The phone ID indicated it was Marc Harper. Since the counting room was a part of the Mosque, Omar had to go outside to take the call. No phone conversations were ever allowed inside the Mosque. No one was even allowed to bring a phone into the Mosque. Omar was always the exception.

By the time he got outside of the Mosque the call stopped. There was no voice mail left. What Marc had to say would not have been appropriate over voice mail. Omar went into his recent phone calls in his cell phone and located Marc's number and pushed Marc's name. Marc's phone rang on his Bluetooth as he was driving to his football game. The phone ID on his screen read a number he didn't know, but it had to be Omar returning his call. This was the moment he dreaded. He pushed the phone button on his steering wheel.

"Hello Mr. Omar."

"I told you only to call me if it was a life or death situation. Is this one of your burner phones?"

"No, I am on my own cell phone."

Omar hung up.

Marc really got scared. He pulled over to the side of the road and took out one of his burner phones that he carried in his glove compartment. He dialed Omar's burner number.

"Mr. Omar, I am so sorry, but this may be one of those life or death situations. I just received a call from Harrison Ramsey. There was a confrontation on the beach in Aruba a day or two ago between Brad Nickolas and Kelly Walker. She refused to give him the most recent funds to be deposited. Her husband, Bob, intervened and there was a skirmish."

"I don't understand. Did she have the funds with her when Nickolas met her?"

"I don't know."

"So figure it out. I want to know what happened and where's my half million dollars? And don't ever call me again on your cell phone."

"I am so sorry about that sir. But it's a little more complicated than that. Irving may have killed one of his co-custom workers"

"Who was murdered?"

"Some man named Ruiz, I think"

"Johm Ruiz?

"I think that was his name."

"I told you no one was to be murdered in this matter. Those complications are now for you and Ramsey to handle. I had nothing to do with any murder. Now, I want to know why Johm was murdered. He was a good person. Call me when the transfer is complete. It needs to be in the accounts by tomorrow. And find out about Ruiz."

"So Ruiz is working for you?"

Omar hung up.

Now Marc was really confused. Omar knew Ruiz? Omar recognized the name Brad Nickolas? His good friend Kelly was on the run. This was not good. Marc thought, what do I do next?

Alle awoke at 9:30 AM. Kaydra was still sleeping. The last several days were draining. Alle knew that Kaydra hadn't had a good meal for days. First, she heard that her father had been murdered. Then she heard he died of natural causes. Nonetheless, Johm was dead. Alle was overwhelmed by all of this also. Alle wondered how and why Dr. Fingal would sign the death certificate indicating Johm died of natural causes. She knew better. Johm and Alle had been going together for several years. Omar had many contacts and could arrange anything. Alle really loved Johm, but he was slowly becoming very different. Whenever they spoke about marriage, Johm started to emotionally abuse her? What had she done? She was afraid that it may even turn into physical abuse. However, she was torn. What a bad thought about someone she loved.

Now she and Kaydra had to meet a mortician who would arrange for Johm to be cremated. Kaydra never knew that it took a special burial permit to have a loved one buried in Aruba. The permit usually took months for approval and arrangements had to be made before one dies. How would she even know that? Her father wasn't old. They never spoke about that. Also, Kaydra and her mother could never really communicate very well. The issue of death never really came up. Kaydra lived in Aruba all her life until she left for college. She had met thousands of American tourists, but never traveled to the United States. Her mother went there often, but, Kaydra was never included. Even her father wasn't included. Now she lives in North Carolina. She even married another man, but Kaydra heard that it didn't last long. Kaydra hated her mother and never understood her mother's relationship with her father.

Once Kaydra moved to Florida to go to school her vision of the world became different. Living in Gainesville, Florida, was a completely different life. Kaydra believed that her father had saved for years to make sure his daughter was well educated. At least she thought that was the only way he could afford to pay for her education. Now, she was making arrangements to have him cremated. She hated that. She wanted her father to have a burial grave so she could go there and speak with him. But it was what it was. What about her father's ex-wife? Should Kaydra call her? After all she was her mother. Could Kaydra ever believe that she may have been involved somehow? But those questions would have to wait for another day.

Alle decided to fix her and Kaydra a large breakfast meal. Luckily Johm had plenty of food in his refrigerator. Three eggs, for each of them, cooked over medium, three strips of crispy bacon, a bowl of fresh fruit cut up in small cubes, a toasted bagel with cream cheese and a glass of orange juice. While she was preparing the feast, a hot pot of coffee was brewing.

Kaydra awoke smelling something very delicious.

She pulled herself out of her own bed, put on her robe, threw some cold water on her face and walked out to the kitchen.

"Oh my God! You are my savior. I am starved. How did you know?"

"I loved Johm, but he was your father. You have gone through Hell these last several days. I thought you needed something substantial to eat. After all we have a tough day ahead of us."

"Nothing could have been more perfect."

Both women knew they had an appointment at the Olive Tree Funeral Home at 1:30. So they had time to enjoy a full homemade meal together and to gather themselves for what was ahead that day. They both leisurely finished their breakfast, left the dishes and pans in the sink and each took a shower.

At 12:00 both women got into Alle's car and started driving to San Nicholas to meet the mortician to make arrangements for Kaydra's father. On the way they discussed what kind of a celebration of life they should plan for the man who was loved by many and who was the love of both woman's lives.

That same morning Dr. Fingal was doing his rounds with his two residents at the Dr. Horacio Oduber Hospital. He was still upset that Harrison Ramsey had to escort him out of the casino when he felt his luck may had been changing. However, if Ramsey was willing to take the chance of getting caught by his bosses to wipe off nearly a hundred thousand dollars of losses, then the forging of a toxicology and autopsy report should be worth a lot more. What really happened to Johm Ruiz? There was never any real toxicology report. Fingal had no idea what Ramsey was into but it must be something big to have Ruiz killed, or at least cover up who actually may have murdered him.

Perhaps a meeting with Harrison to discuss another line of credit at the casino may be one way to find out how big of a venture Harrison was really involved in. Fingal decided that an appointment with Harrison may be prudent. Fingal was smart and had learned to read people over his years as a physician. A man to man discussion with Harrison may be not only appropriate, but also lucrative. The urge to gamble is intoxicating. The worse Harrison could say would be no. If he does, Fingal thought that he could threaten to go to Harrison's bosses concerning his illegal venture. Fingal has bluffed his way through life for years. That's all part of his gambling addiction. But snitching on Harrison would also cause Fingal to pay back the hotel his losses and worse even have him arrested. However the gambling urge was more important. When he completed his rounds, he made that call to Harrison.

CHAPTER 8

Kelly was walking very fast through the high rise district of Aruba. When she got to the Hyatt Hotel and went inside. Her first stop was the woman's clothing store. She took several hundred dollars out of the black leather bag she was carrying. She purchased two tops, several pairs of leggings, some under garments and a pair of shoes. Next she went to the sundry store and purchased two burner phones.

She knew there were security cameras everywhere in the hotel. Eventually she was certain they would determine she had been at the Hyatt. But that would take some time. She would be long gone by then. Next, she went to the cab stand and had the valet call her a cab from the line of cabs waiting on the ramp to the entrance of the hotel. The valet blew his whistle and a small Toyota Corona cab drove up the ramp to the hotel entrance.

"Where can I tell the driver you are going miss?" asked the valet.

"I'll tell the driver, thanks," as she gave the valet a five dollar bill as a tip. Kelly knew that the cabs all charged flat fees by zone. A ride from the high rise area to the airport was $27.00.

Kelly got in the cab, took out two $20 bills, and told the driver she wanted to go to the airport and be let out at the American Airlines check in area. It took the cab about 30 minutes to get to the airport. Kelly said nothing to the cab driver. She usually chatted with every cab driver she encountered on the Island. In fact many times she had the same cab driver due to the number of times her and her husband took cabs. They never rented a car. Many drivers remembered them and would have a conversation about how they were doing on their vacation. Kelly also asked questions about the cabbies family and life on the Island. Luckily Kelly had never seen this cab driver. Hopefully he wouldn't remember her. Kelly paid the cab driver the $40.00 she had in her hand which included a nice tip. She got out of the cab and secured a place in the check in line for American Airlines. When it was her turn to check in, Kelly indicated that she wanted to purchase a first class one way ticket on the next plane to Miami.

"May I see your passport?" asked the airline clerk.

Kelly took out a passport indicating her name was Krista Mills with a Boca Raton, Florida, address. The picture on the passport was Kelly's. It was a perfect fake US passport.

"How do you want to pay for your ticket?"

"Cash, how much is it?"

$1,145.00."

Kelly counted out 11 hundred dollar bills, two twenties and a five dollar bill. The clerk recounted the money and then printed out the ticket in the name of Krista Mills.

"Do you have any luggage to check?"

Kelly answered that she only had a carry on. The clerk gave Kelly her ticket and directed her towards Aruba customs. Kelly now began to get a little stressed. Most of the custom officers knew both her and Bob.

Kelly followed the red line put down by the airport in order to make following the correct procedures through both Aruba and US customs easier. All other countries had a yellow line to follow. From the American Airlines ticket counter, Kelly went through an electric double door that opened automatically. She approached an Aruba custom employee sitting behind a table. Luckily she was at the airport late in the evening. Her and Bob usually arrived and departed Aruba early in the morning or afternoon. The evening custom officers would be ones she most likely had not encountered.

"Passport and ticket please."

Kelly didn't recognize him. She gave him her passport and ticket to Miami. The man looked at the passport picture and then looked at Kelly. He thought that he had seen her before. But her name didn't ring any bells. He approved her and sent her on to the metal detectors and the x-ray machine for carry-ons. As she went through the metal detector and her black bag went through the x-ray machine, Kelly was looking for Irving. He was nowhere in sight. Usually he handled customs for incoming travelers. Her stress level went down.

Next she continued to follow the red line to go through US customs. Again no problem there. The agent asked her the usual questions including if she was carrying any cash over $10,000.00. He asked several other usual questions that were asked to every US traveler. She lied on only the questions dealing with her name and the cash. They never checked her bag. Not unusual. Aruba was a tourist haven and they never wanted to inconvenience US traveler unless there was obviously something not normal. Kelly, except for the fact that she was traveling alone, was very normal.

Once Kelly cleared both customs she walked towards her gate for the trip to Miami. She passed dozens of retail stores all selling souvenirs, duty free liquor, perfumes, chocolates and other miscellaneous item. She passed many food kiosks, but didn't buy any food since she knew that she would get food in the first class section on the plane. She hadn't eaten in hours.

Forty minutes after arriving at the gate, the first class travelers were the first called to board the plane. Kelly got on the flight and took her seat next to the window in seat 3A. She immediately ordered a glass of champagne. No one questioned her identity at any point through the entire process. Twenty minutes later her plane took off and Kelly was on her way to Miami with over a half million dollars in the overhead compartment.

Alle and Kaydra arrived at the Olive Tree Funeral Home just after 1:30 PM. They asked the receptionist to see the director, Yusuf Gurey.

"Mr. Gurey is currently with a client. He should be available in an hour or so," responded the receptionist.

Alle and Kaydra looked surprised.

"Biob Peterson, the Chief of Police specifically made an appointment with me at 1:30 today to discuss arrangements for my father, Johm Ruiz," replied Kaydra.

The receptionist looked at Mr. Gurey's calendar for the day.

"You are correct Ms....."

"Ms. Kaydra Ruiz, Johm Ruiz's daughter."

"There must be some misunderstanding. Another woman came in about 30 minutes before you and said she had an appointment with Mr. Gurey concerning Mr. Ruiz. I never looked at the calendar. I just assumed she had the appointment. Let me get Mr. Gurey on the phone and see if we can straighten this out."

The receptionist called the conference room where Mr. Gurey was with the client. She explained the situation to him and then she hung up.

"Mr. Gurey will be out in a moment. Please have a seat."

Alle and Kaydra couldn't understand what exactly caused this mix up. Within two minutes a middle aged woman, dressed in an expensive Channel all-black suit with a light green blouse came out to the reception area with Mr. Gurey. Both Alle and Kaydra looked at the woman for several seconds before they recognized her.

"Mother, what in the Hell are you doing here?" asked Kaydra.

"I am so sorry Ms. Ruiz," said Mr. Gurey. "When I got the call from Chief Peterson I must have misunderstood as to which Ms. Ruiz I would be meeting today."

"How in the world did you know about this meeting? But more important why in Hell are you here?" uttered Kaydra to her mother as she started to cry. "You and dad haven't communicated for years. And even if you had, what rights do you have for any input into my father's last arrangements. You have had nothing to do with him in years. You don't even know about my life or anything important in my life. It's been over 6 years since you divorced my father for that other asshole of a man. I want you out of here now."

"I know that I should have called you before I came. That's my fault and I do apologize. But there are a couple of matters you need to understand."

Alle was calmly still in her chair and listing to Natasha attempting to calm down her daughter. She also was somewhat surprised as Kaydra. But that was for different reasons.

"You are correct about the man who enticed me to leave your father. He was a big mistake. I never should have married him. After we moved to the States he became very abusive, both emotionally and physically. I divorced him years ago and took back your father's name. So I am still Natasha Ruiz. Your father and I have been communicating over the last several years or so. Obviously he never told you."

"What the Hell does that mean?" barked Alle trying to convince Kaydra that Alle really hadn't spoken to Natasha, from time to time. "Johm never mentioned the fact that you and he started speaking again. I have been with him for over two years and not once did he say he talked to you," lied Alle.

"Alle, there was nothing romantic going on between me and Johm. Our talks were my way of apologizing to him about the way I treated him years ago. I just didn't want him to hate me for the rest of his life," lied Natasha only because her daughter was listening, but Alle understood.

Natasha continued looking at Kaydra, "I even attempted to get his blessing to be able to communicate with you, Kaydra. He loved you very much. He made that very clear to me. He wouldn't allow any contact. He knew how you felt about me. But, I still wanted to keep up on what was happening in your life. If I called you on my own, I knew you wouldn't speak with me. So, your father kept me updated as to what was happening in your life, honey. I know you're attending the University of Florida. You're starting your junior year and majoring in Hospitality Administration. I understand you want to come back to the Island and work for a hotel or restaurant. I know you have no steady beau. I wish you did, but I wanted to know everything. After all, you are still my daughter."

"And how did you know about dad? And that he would be here today at this time?" asked Kaydra.

"Biob Peterson and I have always been good friends. You knew that. He called me and told me about Johm. He also told me that you would be here at 1:30 and thought that maybe if we met under these circumstances it may be a way to possibly heal some of the wounds between us. I would very much like that to happen."

Alle got up from her seat and took Kaydra aside. She put her arm around her waist and told her that she was as surprised to see Natasha there as Kaydra was. However, Alle emphasized that her mother seemed sincere about what she was trying to tell her. She was her mother and she, like all mothers, wanted the best for her daughter. Alle lied when she said that she had no idea that her father and mother had been speaking, but Alle was certain how her father felt about her. She believed Natasha when she said that there was no romantic feelings between them. Alle knew that would never happen again. However, she did have some instinct that Johm may have, in some way, been updating Natasha about Kaydra. Alle suggested that at least, through the funeral, it may be a good opportunity for her and her mother to try to tolerate each other. After that, they both could let things go where it may.

Natasha waited patiently while Alle and Kaydra spoke. When they were done, Natasha went over to Kaydra and started to hug her. Kaydra flinched and moved away.

"Mother, I am still not pleased you're here, but I am attempting to try to understand. At least a little. I will agree to be civil with you through this ordeal. But I will be the one to make the arrangements. You can have no say. After the funeral is completed, maybe we can talk, but no promises."

"I can't ask for any more than that. I love you Kaydra and I would love to be back in your life. But I will accept your decision on that issue," as Natasha started to tear up fake tears. "I know that it has been hard for your father to help you out with your tuition and costs at school. Actually, I have no idea where he got the money. One thing I did receive from that asshole of a man I divorced in North Carolina was a lot of money. I really want to help with the costs of the cremation and the celebration of your father's life. I know some important people at the downtown Radisson. Let me help with the costs. You can make all the arrangements. But can I at least help cover the costs?"

Kaydra looked at Alle who immediately smiled. Kaydra continued to look at Alle and there was a long pause. Alle finally looked at Natasha and said that both she and Kaydra would appreciate Natasha's kindness.

Then Alle and Kaydra followed the silent Mr. Gurey into the conference room to finalize Johm Ruiz's arrangements. Natasha left the mortuary with a small hope that she and Kaydra would have some sort of relationship after the celebration of life. However, she was never going to tell Kaydra how her father acquired the funds to send her to school. She was surprised Alle didn't flinch when that comment came up. That would have devastate Kaydra.

CHAPTER 9

Detectives Franken and Geil watched the hotel security tape of Kelly several times. They then had a chat as to whether or not they should label this case as a missing or abducted person matter or a runaway. Usually a runaway deals with a minor, but they didn't have any clue what else to call this unusual set of facts. They were unaware of the scheme that Kelly was involved in, or that there was any money missing. For all they knew, Kelly just wanted to leave her husband.

They both remembered the media circus atmosphere that went on when Natalee Holloway was abducted. The international publicity concerning Aruba set back tourism for several years. Neither detective wanted that to happen again. Both were certain that neither did their Chief nor did anyone else involved in the tourism trade.

They had to make a decision. A missing or abducted person would bring in Federal law enforcement from the United States since Kelly was an American citizen. Also, the Netherlands police would intervene to help out the FBI. On the other hand, neither detective could determine if a crime actually occurred. They discussed having the police stay out of Kelly's disappearance until someone could point to a specific crime committed by Kelly. They knew that her husband would argue that point, but if there was a crime being perpetrated maybe Bob or Harrison could enlighten them. They both liked that idea.

Harrison and Bob were in Harrison's office while the detectives reviewed the security tapes. Harrison decided to bring Bob in to explain and update him on exactly what was happening with him, Kelly, Marc

Harper and Irving Wernet. Bob was furious. Not because of their involvement in the scheme, but because no one had the courtesy to let him in on this much earlier. After all they were just helping Omar launder some money from his fund raising duties. Someone skimming off the top isn't that unusual. However, if Omar was threatening their lives, he should have known about it. Bob wondered, why leave him out of what was going on? Why didn't his best friend or wife trust him? It didn't sound like something very complicated. Maybe a little criminal, but they were under duress. So why?

"Bob, both Kelly and I knew that if we told you up front, you would have insisted that we immediately inform the authorities in Minneapolis or Aruba."

"I would have. Now we're all criminals. Is there an end game here? When will Omar let you stop this scheme? I don't care how much money you all are making. I don't want to go to jail. I am really pissed. Now tell me where in the Hell is Kelly? You must know."

"On my mother's grave, I have no idea. I know she wasn't happy about what we were doing, but I am sure that the incident on the beach scared the crap out of her. What she may think as to what she can do about it, I don't know. But I will contact Marc Harper and see what may be going on and what may be in Omar's mind. Most important I need to find out if Kelly has deposited the money in the offshore accounts."

As Harrison and Bob were finishing their talk, detectives Franken and Geil knocked on Harrison's door. Harrison motioned for them to come in.

Bob was the first to confront the detectives. "So what's the plan to find my wife? You had your CSI people scrub my hotel room. You have scoured the hotel and you have reviewed the security tapes for an hour. What's your conclusion? And how can we help?"

"Gentlemen," started the senior detective, "this is a strange set of circumstances. Our CSI personnel found nothing incriminating. What we thought may be some blood was just some dried makeup. There were no fingerprints other than Ms. Walker's or yours, Mr. Walker. The disarray in the room seemed staged. Ms. Walker's purse, wallet, passport, money and keys left in the room is a mystery. The security tape just shows a woman who is Ms. Walker or someone closely resembling Ms. Walker leaving the hotel room with a black bag that looked like a large doctor's bag. What was in that bag we have no idea. None of Ms. Walker's clothes were missing. Mr. Walker you confirmed that fact. Also, after speaking with the head of security for your hotel, Mr. Ramsey, they found nothing incriminating either."

"So what the Hell does that all mean?" asked Bob. "Those tapes definitely showed my wife leaving the hotel. So what is your plan to find her?"

Harrison listened to the conversation between the detectives and Bob and he had a feeling that this was not going to end well for anyone. He thought about saying something to the detectives as to what they should probably do next, but the last thing that he or Bob wanted was to reveal anything about the scheme that was currently in progress. So he just waited for the detective's response to Bob's questions.

"Mr. Harrison and Mr. Walker, both Esmar and I believe that something strange is happening," maintained Franken. "However, neither of us can positively determine that any crime has occurred. We don't know Ms. Walker, but we believe the two of you when you told us that the woman in the security tape was Kelly Walker. There is nothing criminal about a woman leaving her hotel room in the fashion we witnessed on the tape or by examining the hotel room. There could be a dozen reasons for her leaving as she did. No offense to you Mr. Walker, but you could be abusing her and this was her way of getting out of a bad marriage."

"That is ridiculous! I can't believe you would even think, let alone say that about me you son of a bitches."

"Please, Mr. Walker, we are not accusing you of anything. We are just trying to communicate to you that since we cannot find any crime that was perpetrated by Ms. Walker, or you Mr. Walker, we are not going to open a file on this matter, at least for now. We have spoken to our Chief and he agrees with us. If you want to call him, please feel free to do so."

"So that's it?" uttered Bob.

Detective Franken looked at both Bob and Harrison and observe their disappointment and distain. Then Franken spoke to the two unhappy men.

"As a courtesy to the Marriott Hotel, whose employees and owner have supported this Island's police over the years, and the Walkers who frequent our Island so often, our Chief has agreed to let us do some investigation in the high rise area to see if we can locate your wife, Mr. Walker. We will take the picture you gave us of your wife and her passport and canvas all the hotels and, retail stores, and cab companies to see if anyone has seen her or may know of her whereabouts. We will start first thing in the morning and spend the day on that investigation. If we find anything about her disappearance we will let you both know."

"God bless you," replied Bob. "I will wait for your call."

With that pledge, the detectives left. They felt bad for Bob Walker, but their hands were tied. Both detectives thought that the next day would be some time well spent, but they were not optimistic. What they saw on that security tape showed them someone who wanted out of something and fast. They had no idea why.

Krista Mills, also known as Kelly Walker, landed at the Miami airport about 1:05 AM very early the next morning. She was exhausted. She walked the long concourse to the cab stand outside the airport. She hailed a cab and asked the driver the closest upscale hotel from the airport.

"There is the Marriott Airport Hotel just less than a mile."

"No not that one. I don't like Marriott's," lied Kelly. She didn't want to go to a brand that had her and her husband in their computers. They were both Marriott Hotel Bovoy Club members. "How about the next closest one?"

"There is a Great Western Garden Hotel just a mile away. I hear it's very nice," said the cab driver in a Latino accent.

"Sounds good. Take me there."

When they arrived about 10 minutes later, Kelly got out of the cab, paid him in cash with a nice tip and walked into the hotel. She approached the check in desk and asked for a single for the night. She indicated that she didn't have a reservation.

"No problem," said the clerk who had just awakened from a light nap. "May I see your identification and a credit card?"

Kelly took out her passport that identified her as Krista Mills. "I don't have a credit card. My purse was stolen yesterday. I will pay cash."

"Ms. Mills, without a credit card we will have to hold your passport until you check out. Incidentals you know."

"No problem," answered Kelly.

Kelly signed in, gave the clerk her passport and paid the room charge for a night in cash. She proceeded to the room and immediately went to the hotel's phone and dialed a long distance call to St. Paul Minnesota. It was an hour earlier there but Marc Harper and his wife were asleep. The phone rang three times. Finally Marc answered the phone.

"Who is this calling at this hour?"

"Marc, it's me, Kelly. I need to speak with you."

"Kelly, aren't you in Aruba. Let me go in the other room. I don't want my wife to wake up."

As Marc walked into his family room, he said, "Kelly, what the Hell is going on? Have you given the money to Brad Nickolas so it could be deposited tomorrow? You know Omar's rules.

"No, I have it all with me. I am in Miami registered under an alias. I am at the Great Western Garden airport hotel. I will be flying to Minneapolis tomorrow morning."

"That is bad news. Harrison called me and told me that you and the money were missing. Omar will know that the money hasn't been deposited in a day or two. What are you doing? You know the consequences of stealing from Omar."

"I have a plan. I believe there is something unusual going on with Omar. Can you pick me up at the airport tomorrow? I have no idea which flight I'll be on so I will call your cell when I arrive."

"I have school tomorrow, but will you text me when you get in. I don't allow cell phones in my classroom. I don't want any student to know I have mine. Where are we going from there?"

"My house. We can talk there. Bob is still in Aruba. He probably has the police looking for me."

"I have no idea what you are doing, but I'll be there about 45 minutes after I get your text even if I have to dismiss my class."

"Great. I miss you. We need to talk about a lot. See you tomorrow."

Kelly then hung up. Marc sneaked back in bed. "Who was that at this hour? Asked Marc's wife.

It was my principal. A special meeting has been set for all of the teachers on some important matter he wouldn't tell me about. I don't know when I'll be home tomorrow. So go back to sleep."

Marc's wife thought the call at midnight was very strange, but she said nothing and went back to bed. She would quiz him when he got home after school the next day.

Kelly got up late the next morning about 10:00 AM. She took a shower and used the toiletries in the room to wash her hair and face. There was a hair dryer in the room. She put on some new clothes she purchased at the Hyatt Hotel the day before. She went down to the lobby to use their computer to find the next direct Delta flight to Minneapolis/St. Paul. It was at 2:00 PM. She went back to her room and gathered her black leather bag and grabbed a cab to the airport.

Once she arrived at the airport she went to the Delta check in counter and asked for a first class one way ticket to the Twin Cities on the 2:00PM flight.

"May I see some identification please?"

Kelly took out her passport and handed it to the Delta agent. The name on the passport was Ana Bannen with a St. Louis Missouri address. The picture on the passport was Kelly's. It was another perfect fake US passport. The Delta agent looked at the picture and then back at Kelly.

"How would you like to pay for the ticket Ms. Bannen?"

"Cash. How much is it?"

$955.00."

Kelly paid with 9 hundred dollar bills a 50 dollar bill and a 5 dollar bill. The agent told Kelly there was only one first class seat left. It was seat number 5D. Kelly had no problem. The Delta agent told her to go to the Delta concourse, gate G16. Kelly took the shuttle to Delta concourse G, gate 16 just in time for boarding with the first class ticket holders.

Kelly went to seat 5D and immediately ordered a glass of champagne. Twenty minutes later the plane was full and took off for the Twin Cities. Again, no one questioned Kelly about anything at any time.

CHAPTER 10

Diric Omar's illegal operation within 'Little Mogadishu' and in several other locations throughout Minneapolis and St. Paul was flourishing according to his right Hand man, Brad Nickolas. With the city councils and the mayors of both cities advocating and passing ordinances that defunded the police and decriminalized "victimless" crimes, it was unlikely that Omar's finance fund raising scheme would be investigated. Omar and others were counting on that.

Over the 25 years Omar had been the finance director for the Masjid Darul-Quba Mosque he has only been operating his illegal operations for the last several years. Everything before that had all been legitimate. However, since the finance director changed to illegal operations, his organization had become over a $5 million enterprise per year. Of that money, half of a million dollars was used for the upkeep of the Mosque including salaries for the people who maintained it. Another $75,000.00 was distributed throughout 'Little Mogadishu' and other Somali neighborhoods in the Twin Cities and St. Cloud, Minnesota, for neighborhood festivals, religious schools and scholarships for Somali young men for college. Omar payed combined salaries of nearly four hundred thousand dollars for his muscle men who handled the security for businesses, employees of his loan sharking business and his gambling business.

Omar pocketed for himself over three and a half million dollars a year, all of which was still located in over 10 off shore banks in the Caribbean and was just lying there acquiring interest. Omar kept $1,000.00 a week for his own living and recreational expenses. The rest of the money went to people who he had demanded, over time, to do him favors. Those favors include movement of operational funds from various locations in Minnesota to Aruba, then to St. Martin, St. Johns and Nassau. Those funds were then moved from those accounts to other Caribbean Island Banks in untraceable offshore numbered accounts. Then the funds were again transferred to one of 10 other offshore untraceable accounts on various other Caribbean Islands. All of the deposits, other than in Aruba banks, and all transfers were performed exclusively by Brad Nickolas. No one else, including Omar, had access to the accounts. Omar trusted Brad and wanted complete plausible deniability.

All of the people who did favors for Omar including Alle Thiel, Marc Harper, Harrison Ramsey, Kelley Walker, Irving Wernet and the late Johm Ruiz also received funds for their favors. Their money was received when Brad decided to send the money by wire transfer to specific numbered accounts in a private bank in Aruba. Each had their own account number. There was no set schedule when their money would arrive. Brad had complete control.

There were 50 other reluctant individuals who were located outside of Aruba and Minnesota who were intimidated into doing favors for other finance directors at Mosques located in several large cities in the US and different Caribbean Islands. Their crimes were much more destructive, harmful and traumatizing than those by Omar. Brad made sure of that.

In the years that Omar's financing turned illegitimate, few person had been seriously harmed. That fact was not known by any other finance directors of the other Mosques that were located outside of Minnesota. None of the people who did favors for any of the other finance directors knew the people who were doing favors for each of those directors. That was intentional by all finance directors. However, recently one of the persons associated with Omar died. John Ruiz. That fact circulated between all of those criminal finance directors. The murder of a person doing favors was very unusual.

Brad Nickolas, who was Omar's major contact concerning the scheme, had a profile on every person who did Omar's favors. He knew their life stories. Where they were born and raised. Where they went to school. Where they work. Their supervisors and co-workers. Who their immediate family members were. Where they all lived, and other intimate secrets. Each of those people know that if they didn't do what was required by them through Omar or Brad, each family member, friend or co-worker of theirs may be in jeopardy. Murder, however, was not the customary threat Omar used as persuasion. The threat of torture and disfigurement was more his style. At least that is what had been told to each of the people doing Omar's favors. That was until the death of John Ruiz.

Immediately thereafter, Kelly was supposedly threatened on the beach by Brad. But Kelly, in retrospect, was never actually threaten. Bob was the one who believed the event on the beach that day was an uncompromising threating gesture. Kelly actually felt like the alleged threat was some type of hoax. Brad actually slipped several fake US passports into Kelly's fanny pack. She was confused. That was because Johm Ruiz's death was a total mystery to Kelly. How and why did he die? Why did Brad give her the passports? She felt that something else, other than the scheme they were all involved with, was actually happening. She needed to find out. What better way than to take half million dollars and retain it instead of having it transferred by Brad Nickolas for depositing it in one of their offshore banks. She knew the consequences if she was wrong. All of her family and friends, including her husband, would be in serious harm. But Kelly believed in her instincts. Now that she was in St. Paul, she knew that if things were to go bad, she could quickly get in touch with Brad Nickolas, or even Omar, and give them the money, or what was left of it.

When Brad Nickolas heard from Omar that he had spoken to Marc, and that Kelly had taken half a million dollars of their money and Johm Ruiz was dead, he had an idea. He would attempt to contact Ruiz's home. Alle would probably answer and he could frighten her enough to see what was happening in Aruba. He needed to answer to Omar. When the phone rang at Ruiz's home Kaydra answered.

"May I speak with Johm please?" asked Brad knowing that he was dead.

"Who is this? Is this some type of joke? If it is, it's not funny," answered Kaydra. Brad was surprised that Alle didn't answered the phone.

Knowing Ruiz was dead, Brad was prepared to frighten Alle. Somehow, he was sure she had something to do with Ruiz's death. She was the one who told Ruiz about her part in the scheme without his or Omar's permission. Johm was then required, as was Irving Wernet, to allow Kelly and Bob to go through customs without any inspections. Alle knew that once Johm was recruited, the money Johm would be receiving from Omar would be much needed by him for his daughter's education. They both spoke about the scheme and the money, even though that was against the rules. Alle's part of the scheme was much less important than Johm's. Alle didn't care. Johm could use all of his money from Omar to fund his daughter's college costs.

Brad found out, through certain connections, that Ruiz was using his compensation to send his daughter to college. But he and Omar needed to know what really happened to Ruiz. Neither one had ordered Ruiz's death. They wouldn't have done that under any circumstances, even though Ruiz was not fully vented when he accidently came into the scheme. Brad was somewhat delighted that Ruiz's money was at least going for a good cause. That assured his silence. In Brad's mind, the others were just greedy, even though that may not have been the case. They were all mostly scared. Brad's call was to find out if Alle may have mentioned something to Ruiz's daughter about how her father was funding her schooling. That also was against the rules. Big time. But not big enough to kill him. Hence the call.

"Kaydra, I am a friend of your father's. I would like to speak with him please."

Kaydra was surprised whoever was on the phone knew her name.

"My father passed away several days ago. Who is this?"

"Johm is dead? How did this happen?" Brad was acting surprised.

"Tell me who this is or I am going to hang up."

"I am so sorry for your loss, Kaydra. Is Alle there?"

"Who is this? How do you know my father and Alle? Do you know my mother too?"

Brad hung up. He felt that Kaydra was unaware of what was actually happening. But he still needed information as to what Alle knew about Ruiz's death. There were other ways.

Kaydra didn't understand what just happened. It scared her. So she called Alle, but her phone went to voice mail. Kaydra left a message. "Alle give me a call as soon as you can. I just received a strange call concerning my father. I need to speak with you."

Alle heard her phone ring and knew that Kaydra was leaving a message. She couldn't answer the phone since she was on a burner phone with Diric Omar.

"What is this about Johm being dead? What happened?" asked Omar.

"He passed due to a non-diagnosed aneurysm in his brain. He was found at his home on the floor of his kitchen by the police when he didn't show up for work."

"Do you believe that, Alle?"

"One of the best doctors on the Island did the autopsy and toxicology tests. His final report indicated that was the cause of death."

"I don't believe that. You were the one who recruited Johm, even though I told you that your work was to be strictly confidential between you, me, Irving and Brad Nickolas. What did you do to Johm? You know I actually liked him. I had dinner with him once in Minneapolis. Dr. Burton Woodcock had Johm flown to Minneapolis from Aruba. They were acquaintances. Johm helped him many times through customs whenever he went to Aruba on vacation. He was faithful and honest with me when I spoke with him on the phone. Rare traits in my business. And he used his money to fund his daughter's schooling. I admire that. You, however, have been difficult since the day I met you. Chasing off to Aruba after you left my office building. When I finally needed that favor, it took my security people over three weeks to find you. That was scarce. You must have ways to deflect persons from gaining information about your movements. I have a file on your family and friends, as well as Johm's daughter and many of his friends and ex-wife. So tell me the truth. Did you do it for greed? Where you tired of making less money than Johm? You could have spoken with Brad or me about it. He, at least, used his money for a good cause. You just liked to buy expensive things.

Pure greed. I am surprised Johm never questioned your purchases. You can't be making a lot of money working in that woman's health clinic. So what really happen?"

"Mr. Omar, I know the consequences of lying to you and attempting to evade you. I would never do that. I love my family and Johm and Kaydra too much. You have to believe me. I didn't know you knew him. You should have told me. I only know what the autopsy showed. And you don't pay me enough money to buy expensive things. Kaydra is having Johm cremated tomorrow and we have a celebration of life planned for Johm at the downtown Radisson the next day. You must believe me. I had nothing to do with Johm's death." Alle was getting scared and nervous for lying.

"I will believe you only if you do two things for me."

"Anything," she was now really frightened.

"First, stop Kaydra from having Johm's body cremated. I have a fine doctor friend that will be in Aruba tomorrow. You know his name. Dr. Burton Woodcock. I will get him a room at the Marriott Hotel & Casino. I know the manager of that hotel well. I want my doctor to review the autopsy report, to examine the toxicology report and examine Johm's body. You or Kaydra make the arrangements. He will tell me how Johm really died. If he died as you say he did, I will let this go."

"I can't do that. Johm is Kaydra's father. She won't let some unknown doctor re-examine her father's body or autopsy reports. I know she won't put off his celebration of life."

"Alle, you're a smart and cunning lady. I trust you can come up with something to convince the daughter. No one has to know. The celebration of life can go on as if the body was cremated. After my doctor reviews everything, Johm's body can be cremated. Kaydra's wellbeing depends on you."

"I can try. Now, what's the second favor?"

"I told you I know the manager of the Marriott Hotel. Well, he does favors for me also, from time to time. But you will keep that fact to yourself. Never reveal that to anyone. He knows about some missing money. A lot of money. Tell him that you spoke with me and that he needs to find the money and give me a call. Tell him I want to know why his friend Kelly disappeared with my money. This is more important than Johm's death. If I don't hear from him concerning my money relatively soon, this will be on you. Do you understand what I am saying?"

"Unfortunately I do."

"Good."

Then Omar hung up.

Harrison was on the phone with Dr. Fingal. He wanted to make an appointment to see Harrison about working out another line of credit at the Marriott casino. Harrison was calm during the call and politely refused to discuss anything of the sort with the Doctor. Harrison told him that the deal between them had been completed and he didn't want to see Fingal in the casino unless he had his own money with him. There would be no more credit lines. Fingal thought that it would be in Harrison's best interest if they met and talked it out. Harrison refused. He knew that Fingal would never go to the police about the toxicology report on Ruiz. Fingal's reputation on the Island was his ticket to making the kind of money he was making. He would never take a chance to lose that or his impeccable reputation. He would probably lose his family also.

But Fingal's gambling addiction was deep in his soul. He needed that rush. No other hotel on the Island gave credit lines without a substantial amount of money up front. He always felt that his time to win was now. His losing streak couldn't last much longer. He told Harrison to think about his proposal and he would call Harrison back in a day or two. He reminded Harrison that if he went to the police Harrison's future in the hospitality business was over. Harrison was young and Fingal was near retirement. Fingal believed that he had less to lose. Another bluff by Fingal. Then Fingal hung up. Harrison believed the issue was over. He knew Fingal was only bluffing.

Harrison went back to work. However, that phone call was still in the back of his mind. This entire predicament was due to several naïve college kids attempting to do a good act. Stupid, he thought.

As Harrison was going over the hotel's latest financial reports, Alle Theil knocked on his open door. Harrison had no idea who she was. He thought she must be a guest at the hotel and was coming to complain about something that happened to her or her family during her stay at the hotel. It wouldn't be the first time. Usually complaints first went through the front desk or the concierge before it came to the manager of the hotel. Harrison thought that maybe this matter may be something other than a complaint.

"Come in. My name is Harrison Ramsey. I am the manager of the hotel and casino. May I help you with something?"

"I know who you are. My name is Alle Theil. I was John Ruiz's girlfriend."

"Really. I am so sorry for your loss Ms. Thiel. What is it I can do for you?"

"Actually it's something I can do for the two of us."

Harrison was confused. "What is it that you can do for the two of us?"

"You know a man named Diric Omar. So do I. I just had a frightening phone conversation with him. It seems that a good friend of yours, a person named Kelly, is missing and has some money that belongs to him. He indicated that you and she are friends and that you would be able to tell Mr. Omar where Kelly and his money may be."

"Ms. Thiel, I am not sure what you're talking about. I don't know anyone named Diric Omar. Are you sure you are speaking to the right person?"

"Oh, I'm sure. Omar made it very clear and he inferred the consequences if you couldn't help him."

"Alle, may I call you Alle?

"Please."

"I may know something about what you are talking about. But I'm not really sure. Give me your contact information. I will call you if I find anything out about this Kelly. I wish I could tell you more, but that's the best I can do right now."

"But what about Omar? I have a family. He knows where they are."

"Do you really think Omar had Johm murdered? Harrison finally confessed. As far as I know, I have been involved with him for almost three years now. I don't know of anyone that he has seriously hurt even after they were seriously being threatened."

"Actually, now that you mentioned that, the conversation I had with him makes me believe he doesn't even know who may have killed Johm. And maybe, Johm may not have been murdered," lied Alle.

"You see. There is more to this than either of us know. Just give me your contact information. I promise I will get back with you soon."

"Thank you Harrison."

Alle turned around and left the hotel. She thought about what Harrison had said. But she didn't accomplish her first task. However, she knew what she had to do next.

CHAPTER 11

Detectives Franken and Geil started their short investigation of the disappearance of Kelly Walker the day after she fled her hotel. They had a profile picture of her and her passport picture as well as a picture taken from the security tape which showed her as she was dressed when she left the hotel. They started at the Ritz Carlton Hotel even though that hotel was north of the Marriott. Kelly was seen on the tape traveling south. Kelly was smart. She knew about the hotel's security cameras. So the detectives needed to check if she may have doubled back.

They spoke with the desk clerk, the manager and several other employees to see if they had seen Kelly the night before. Everyone interview indicated that they were not working that late. All of their shifts were morning shifts. Another blunder for the inexperienced detectives. So they requested to view the security tapes for the hotel at the time Kelly disappeared. They viewed the tapes for the entrance to their casino, main entrance and lobby areas for the hotel. No sign of Kelly at the Ritz.

They did this at all of the high rise hotels. They started at the first hotel south of the Marriott, the Holiday Inn, and moved south from hotel to hotel to view each of their security tapes. At 2:00 that afternoon, as they were viewing the security tapes at the Hyatt Hotel, they finally saw Kelly enter the Hyatt at 9:05 the evening before. They followed her into one of the clothing stores and watched her purchase clothing and pack it in the black leather bag she was carrying. She then got into a cab at the entrance of the hotel. The detectives could see the cab number. They immediately called the police station to have their IT assistants look up the owner of the cab and the name and address of the cab driver. Most of the cabs, in Aruba, were private cabs owned by individuals. Under Aruba law, only the owner could drive their cabs.

It only took the IT people just 15 minutes to get back to the detectives with the name and address of the owner of the cab. His name was Ras Filsan. A 45 year old native Aruban who had been driving a cab for 10 years. He worked as a waiter at the most expensive restaurant at the old Radisson Hotel in the high rise district for 10 years in order to save enough money to buy a cab medallion. The cost to purchase a cab medallion was $40,000.00 America money when Filsan purchased his cab license. That was a lot of money for an Aruba native. He still owed his bank nearly $10,000.00 on his loan for the license. He lived in Santa Cruz, a small town in the middle of the Island. Many domestic workers, who worked at tourists venues, or drove cabs, owed small inexpensive homes in that town. The detectives immediately drove to Mr. Filsan's home to question him. When they arrived, Mr. Filsan was just getting ready to start his afternoon and evening shift. He was saying goodbye to his wife. His two children were at school.

As Mr. Filsan was getting into his cab, the detectives drove their car to his driveway and blocked it. They got out of their cars and walked up to Filsan's cab and showed him their badges and credentials. Filsan was terrified. Why would the local police want to question him? His wife started to cry as Filsan looked at her as she was just outside the front door of their home.

"Are you Ras Filsan?" asked detective Franken.

"Yes sir officer, what can I do for you?" answered the terrified cab driver.

"My name is detective Franken and this is my partner detective Geil," as they both showed Filsan their badges and credentials again. "Did you have an occasion to be driving your cab last evening about 9:30?" asked Geil. "By the way, we are not officers, call us detectives," interjected the rookie detective.

"Yes detectives. What is it you need from me?" as Filsan's wife walked over to her husband.

"Did you pick up a fare at the Hyatt Hotel about 9:30 PM? A woman about 35 years old. Here is a picture of her."

"I picked up many fares last night. Maybe 10 or twelve from the Hyatt. I take many tourists from hotel to hotel in the high rise area. They are curious about restaurants, souvenir shops or casinos, in the area. Let me look at her picture again."

The detective showed the cabbie both Kelly's profile picture and the picture from the security tapes.

"I do remember a woman who looked like her. I believe she wanted to go to the airport. I was not very happy since it would be hard to get a return fare to the high rise district at that time of the night."

"Did you take her to the airport or not?"

"Yes, I believe so."

"You believe so? Did you speak with her? Did she tell you where she was flying to? Was she meeting someone at the airport? At which airlines did you leave her off?" as detective Geil fired questions at the frightened cab driver. Filsan's wife was confused. Why did they want to know this? What did her husband do?

"So many questions. I need to think. I had so many fares last night."

"Mr. Filsan, this woman may have committed several very bad crimes. You may be the only person who can identify her and tell us where to find her. Please think."

"Detectives I had no idea that this woman was a criminal. I swear all I did was pick her up at the Hyatt and take her to American Airlines check in at the airport. I can't even remember speaking to her. In fact, all she said to me the entire ride was to let her off at the American Airlines boarding area. Did I do something wrong?"

"Are you certain that this was the lady you picked up at the Hyatt and took to the airport? And your certain you had no conversation with her?" as Franken again showed Filsan Kelly's picture.

"Yes detectives," as Filsan held his wife's arm.

"Thank you Mr. Filsan," answered detective Franken, "We will get back with you if we have any more questions."

"Am I okay? Did I do something wrong? I didn't know this woman," interjected the nervous cabbie.

"We'll call you if we have any more to ask you. Thank you for being so cooperative."

The detectives than left for the airport. Ras and his wife were still scared. They had never spoken with a detective before concerning crimes that may have been committed. Ras thought about taking the day off, but he knew his family needed the money. He kissed his wife and told her that he would be more careful. As he drove away, he still thought he had done something wrong.

The detectives then drove to the airport. They were well acquainted with the airport manager and the custom manager, Coy Dirksz. They went directly to his office to make sure they had his permission to question airline personnel and his custom agents. They explained the situation to Coy. He knew Kelly and her and her husband, Bob. They were frequent flyers. Coy told the detectives that Irving Wernet and Johm Ruiz always took care of them when they flew into the airport and when they left.

"Was that unusual for specific custom agents to help frequent flyers each time they were at the airport?" asked Franken.

"Well, somewhat," answered Coy. "But they were one of a handful of frequent flyers who liked certain custom agents."

"That seems outside the parameters of custom agents responsibilities."

"Why do you say that," asked Coy. "Are you insinuating that something illegal may be going on in customs at this airport?"

"No, just curious."

"Well go ahead and question whomever you wish. You'll find no illegal activities in this airport," arrogantly uttered Coy.

Both detectives than went into the main terminal and approached the American Airline agents. There was a very long line of people with all their luggage waiting to check in. American had 6 check in agents behind the counter. Franken thought they would approach just one at a time and question them about Kelly. He didn't want to make tourists wait any longer than they had to. The airport was always a very busy place. They showed the first agent Kelly's picture and told the agent her name. They asked if they had seen Kelly about 10:00 the night before. They had no luck with the first 4 agents. They didn't even recognize Kelly's name. When they got to the 5th agent, she vaguely recognized Kelly's picture.

"May I see your credentials again?"

Franken took out his badge and credentials and showed them to the agent.

"The woman looks familiar. I believe I saw her sometime yesterday. My shift was 5:00 PM to12:30 AM last night.

"Her name is Kelly Walker," said detective Geil.

"Let me look in my computer and see if I checked her in last night. She really does look familiar. And there is something strange about her, but I can't put my finger on it. I check in hundreds of people every shift."

The agent looked in her computer and typed in Kelly Walker. Nothing came up. She tried her current shift and again nothing came up under that name.

"I guess I didn't check her in yesterday or today. But there is something strange about her face," as the agent pondered her picture for a minute or so. "I do remember something. This woman purchased a one way ticket to somewhere and paid cash. Very few people pay cash. All in 100 dollar bills. But there is no Kelly Walker in the American Airlines computer. Maybe it was someone else who looked like her."

"Don't you check each passenger's passport?"

"Of course. But there is no Kelly Walker who purchased a ticket last night."

"Could she have used another passport with a different name?"

"Not unless it was a forgery, but it would have to have been a very good forgery. I can recognize a forged passport 99% of the time. I have worked here for 12 years and there have been only a handful of forged passports and I caught them all. I have never had a complaint by the authorities of missing a fake passport."

"Do you remember the first or last name of the woman who purchased the one way ticket or even the city she was flying to?"

The agent thought for a minute and said she had no recollection of either.

The detectives thanked the agent and gave her their card and asked her to call them if she remembered anything. Next they moved on to customs. Again no luck. There was one custom agent who thought she looked familiar, but couldn't remember if she went through customs the night before. So the detectives went to see Irving Wernet. He was in his private office getting ready to leave to go to one of the ports of entry.

"Mr. Wernet, May we have a word with you," as detective Franken flashed his badge and credentials.

"I'm in a hurry and a little late, what can I do for you detective..."

"Franken. And this is my partner, detective Geil."

"Do you know this woman?" as he showed him Kelly's picture.

"Sure, that's Kelly Walker. Her and her husband came to the Island a few days ago. Johm Ruiz checked them through. I'm sure you have heard about Johm," sorrowfully said Irving.

"Yes, we are sorry for your loss. Did you see Kelly Walker come through customs last night?"

"No, I wasn't here last night. But if she did come through she would have had to have her picture taken. Everyone has to have their picture taken."

"Oh, really. Do you keep a record of the pictures?"

"Of course. But you need Coy Dirksz's permission. He's the boss."

"He gave us full run of the area and the ability to speak with all employees of the airport and customs."

"Well, okay then. I'll get an agent to bring in last night's pictures with names attached for you to look at. Do you know the approximate time she may have come through?"

"Sometime between 9:00 and midnight."

Irving then left his office and asked one of his agents to bring in last night's pictures of people leaving the Island between 9:00 and midnight. "You can use my office. Good luck." Then Irving went on his way. He was confused. Why would Kelly fly out of Aruba without her husband? Why would she not ask for him to check her through customs? Why were the detectives looking for her? Do they know something about the scheme? He left the airport somewhat frightened.

Franken and Geil spent over three hours looking at hundreds of pictures. They were tired and were sure they were on a cold trail. After all, this was just a curtesy investigation. The custom agent was required to stay in Coy's office while the detectives viewed the pictures. Just before they were about to give up, detective Geil uttered, "George, here she is."

Franken looked at the picture. The time stamp was 10:47 PM. It was Kelly Walker. But the name said Krista Mills. Franken looked again. Maybe it was someone who looked a lot like Kelly. But the detective was sure. It was her. How did she get a passport under that name? Where was she going? They inquired with the custom agent in the office with them.

"Can you tell us what this passenger's destination was?"

"Sure."

The custom agent went into Coy's computer and looked up Krista Mills. "She was on American's last flight to Miami with a one way ticket. That was her final destination."

"Are you certain?"

"Yes sir, detective."

"Would you please print out the photo with the time stamp and the information about her flight?"

"Sure can."

So detectives Franken and Geil got all the information they were looking for. It surprised the daylights out of them. They were certain that it was all going to be a dead end investigation. But it wasn't. But now what? They decided to tell their Chief about their investigation results. But their fear was that they may be on the next flight to Miami. That's the last thing either wanted. Hopefully, the Chief knew someone in Miami that could continue the search. Both detectives thought the same thing, but didn't say it out loud. What the Hell was going on?

CHAPTER 12

After Alle's chat with Harrison about Kelly's disappearance, she drove directly from the Marriott Hotel to the Olive Tree Funeral Home in San Nicolas. She needed to convince Kaydra to allow an unknown doctor from Minneapolis to re-examine her father's body, the autopsy report as well as the toxicology report. How she was going to do that was a mystery in Alle's mind. But, in fact, she really didn't want another doctor to review anything to do with Johm's body. She was still confused with Dr. Fingal's conclusions.

She knew Harrison was not going to reveal anything he may have known about Kelly's disappearance. Omar and Brad Nickolas hinted clearly the threat to her or her family's welfare if she couldn't accomplish the two tasks. But she was trying. She had failed with Harrison on finding out where Kelly and the money may be. But she thought that there were other ways to accomplish that. She pondered what lies she needed to tell Kaydra on her drive to San Nicolas. Alle was beginning to get terrified again.

When Alle arrived at the funeral home, Yusuf Gurey was escorting Chief Biob Peterson, Coy Dirksz and Kaydra Ruiz into a small private room for the last viewing of Johm Ruiz's body prior to cremation. Kaydra couldn't understand why Alle wasn't there. She had told Alle that there would be a final private viewing. Finally, 30 minutes after leaving the Marriott Hotel, Alle ran over to Kaydra as she was walking from the reception area to the viewing room.

"Oh! Thank God. I didn't think you were coming," cried Kaydra to Alle.

"I need to speak with you before you go into the room. It is very important."

"What could be more important than the last time I'll be able to see my father?"

"This is a life or death matter Alle."

"What do you mean life or death? Are you alright? My father is dead."

"I loved your father. I knew him very well. I don't believe he died of an aneurysm. I spoke with a good doctor friend of mine. I told him all the circumstances."

"What are you talking about? Dr. Fingal is an excellent doctor."

"I mean no offense to Dr. Fingal, but according to my friend, there would have been no reason to have a toxicology examination performed if your father died as Dr. Fingal stated."

"Where are you going with this? This doesn't sound like the Alle I know."

"Kaydra, if your father died of a brain aneurysm Fingal would have found it during the autopsy when he examined your father's brain. But, he didn't reach that conclusion until he reviewed the toxicology report. That was a week or so later. My friend told me a toxicology report would not reveal an aneurysm."

"So your point is what?"

"I have made arrangements for my friend to send another coroner from the States to re-examine the autopsy report, your father's body and the toxicology report."

"You got to be kidding. Do you think Dr. Fingal made a mistake? Or, do you think that he intentional misled all of us?"

"I have no idea, but my friend makes a good point. Maybe your father actually died of some kind of foul play?" said Alle in a non-convincing manner. But she knew Omar wanted another autopsy. She was very conflicted.

"No, no. I am not doing this. You need to stop talking like this."

The three men came out of the viewing room and Yusuf asked Kaydra why she hadn't gone in to see her father. Then he saw Alle.

"Hello Ms. Theil. I am glad you finally made it. I wasn't sure you were going to be here. There isn't much time left."

"Mr. Gurey, can the cremation be held up for an extra couple of hours?" asked Alle.

"What in the world for Ms. Theil?"

Just as Mr. Gurey finished speaking with Alle, Dr. Burton Woodcock walked through the front door of the funeral home. He told the receptionist that he was there to view Johm Ruiz's remains.

The receptionist called the phone just outside the viewing room and Yusuf answered the call. He listened to the receptionist's message and his facial expression told Alle what may have just happened.

"Who is this doctor again? And where is he from? Who called him to come here?" asked Yusuf.

Yusuf waited a short while so the receptionist could obtain more information. Then she told Yusuf he was from Minnesota and that Alle Theil asked him to come and reexamine Mr. Ruiz's remains. He also wanted to view the autopsy report and the toxicology report.

"That is impossible," answered Yusuf. "The autopsy report and the toxicology report are at the police station in the morgue."

"What is going on Mr. Yusuf?" asked Kaydra

Yusuf hung up the phone and turned to Alle. "Ms. Theil, did you ask another doctor to reexamine Dr. Fingal's cause of death?"

"I did. I spoke with Kaydra and she has agreed."

"I have done no such thing," exclaimed Kaydra irritably.

"What is going on here Alle?" asked Chief Peterson.

Alle reiterated to the Chief here false reasons for wanting a second doctor to review the autopsy results. All three men were unconvinced with Alle's explanation. As she finished her explanation Dr. Woodcock walked into the hallway.

"Sir, who exactly are you?" asked Chief Peterson.

"My name is Dr. Burton Woodcock. I flew 4,000 miles at the request of Ms. Theil and several other interested persons to give a second opinion on the findings of a Dr. Jan Fingal as to the autopsy of Mr. Johm Ruiz. I was under the impression that you were informed that I would be coming. He is also a friend of mine."

"Alle, is this true?" asked Chief Peterson.

"Yes Biob. How can a second opinion be objectionable? After all, you originally called Johm's death a possible homicide. If Dr. Fingal is correct then all that has happened is just a short pause in the cremation. That doesn't have to change any of the plans for the celebration of Johm's life."

"I believe that I have the final say here. You are speaking about my father's remains," uttered Kaydra.

"Actually Kaydra I have the final say here," said Chief Peterson. "Alle does make a valid point. However, I have no idea who you are Mr. Woodcock. I don't even know if you are really a doctor."

"I can assure you, sir, that I have been a forensic physician for over 30 years. I have all my credentials in my rented vehicle outside. You can view them and make all the calls you desire to confirm my credentials."

"Let me think for a moment," voiced the Chief.

"Ms. Theil, this would be a good time for you to reaffirm that it would be in everybody's best interests that I be allowed to review Dr. Fingal's findings," insisted Dr. Woodcock.

"No need for that," interjected Chief Peterson. "I have made my decision. The cremation will go on as scheduled. I will examine this doctor's credentials and make a few calls. If the doctor is who he says he is, he may review the autopsy report and the toxicology report after the celebration of life has concluded. He can even speak with Dr. Fingal if he wishes. However, a reexamination or new autopsy of Mr. Ruiz's body is out of the question. I have known Dr. Fingal for a long time and I trust him. I have no idea who you are."

"Sir, I urge you to reconsider," pleaded Dr. Woodcock. "An examination of the body is crucial to a second opinion."

"I have made up my mind. You can give me your credentials, Mr. Woodcock, and let me know how to get hold of you after I have confirmed your claims. I also need to confirm who these other interested parties may be."

"Chief, you are making a big mistake," said Alle, again conflicted.

"Leave it be Alle, I now agree with the Chief," firmly said Kaydra.

"Ms. Ruiz, would you like to view your father's remains before I call the hearse to take the body away?" asked Yusuf.

"Of course. Alle do you want to come with me?"

"You are all making a big mistake," articulated Alle. "This decision will come back to haunt all of you."

Alle turned away and quickly left the funeral home. Kaydra was shocked, as she walked into the viewing room for her last glimpse at her father. Why wouldn't Alle want to view the man she was in love with?

Dr. Woodcock went back to the reception room and made a long distance call to 'Little Mogadishu'. After a few minutes on the call he hung up and gathered his credentials and gave them to Chief Peterson. Yusuf waited until Kaydra left the viewing room. He then called the funeral home's hearse for Johm Ruiz's last ride on this earth to the mortuary's crematorium.

Detectives Franken and Geil went to see their Chief in person. The news they had to relate to him was not the type you tell your superior officer over the phone. They explained their entire investigation right up to when she flew away to Miami as Krista Mills. They further indicated that they did this investigation as a good will gesture for a frequent flyer tourist to the Island. No one in Aruba's law enforcement community thought that any crime was perpetrated. But good will generated by the local police, when tourists were involved, always generated good consequences for Aruba. Chief Peterson was not as surprised about the results of his detectives' findings as they thought he would.

The Chief had just witnessed Alle Theil begging to have a second autopsy performed on Johm Ruiz's body. Also, an alleged Minnesota doctor showed up, out of the blue, at the funeral home to perform it. The Chief thought all of that was very strange. Now he heard from his detectives about the circumstances of Kelly Walker's disappearance. Something was going on. The Chief didn't believe in coincidences. Was there some sort of criminal enterprise happening?

"Let me call Houston Cavey of the NCB. He or Cyrus Turnbull may have connections with the FBI. Both have worked with the FBI on several occasions. You remember that they investigated John Ruiz's home after his death," said the Chief. "Maybe they know someone at the Miami FBI that can do some 'off the record' investigating concerning Kelly Walker, or the alias she used, Krista Mills."

"Great idea Chief," happily muttered George Franken. Both detectives really despised the thought of having to fly to Miami.

The Chief picked up his phone and called the NCB. Houston Cavey was there. The Chief explained the entire situation concerning Johm Ruiz and Kelly Walker. At first Houston was apprehensive to get the FBI involved in a matter where no official crimes had been identified, other than maybe forgery of a US passport. But maybe that was enough for at least a call. Houston agreed to call the Miami Director of the FBI, who he knew personally, and see what he had to say.

"I'll get back with you Chief as soon as I speak with Director Miles Hudson."

Detectives Franken and Geil now thought that their role in the investigation was probably over. So they decided to go home and relax with their families. Both were happy to remain in Aruba.

It was less than two hours after George Franken got home when he received a call from Director Miles Hudson.

"Detective George Franken?"

"This is he."

This is Director Miles Hudson of the Miami FBI."

"Yes sir," uttered Franken surprisingly.

"I understand that you have been investigating the disappearance of a Kelly Walker out of St. Paul Minnesota. Also, at the same time you did some investigative work with the NCB concerning the death of a Johm Ruiz."

"Yes sir, however I'm not sure where Kelly Walker lives in the States."

"Does this Kelly Walker have a husband Bob Walker, who is good friends with Harrison Ramsey, the general manager of the Aruba Marriott Hotel & Casino?"

"Why yes sir."

"George, I have spoken with Chief Peterson about this probe. He and I came to an understanding. The FBI would appreciate it if you and your partner would continue on this investigation and cooperate with the FBI. Your Chief has agreed to our mutual cooperation."

"I don't understand Director. I was under the impression that Johm Ruiz's death was due to natural causes. Also, there was a determination that Kelly Walker didn't commit any crime."

"The alleged forgery of a US passport is a Federal offense detective."

"I understand that, but what does that have to do with Aruba or Johm Ruiz's death?"

"George, what I am about to tell you is extremely confidential. Only you, your partner and your Chief will know about this. You can't even tell your wives. Do you understand?

"Yes sir."

"Kelly Walker is a CI for the FBI."

"Kelly Walker is one of your confidential informants?" said Franken utterly overwhelmed.

"Yes, but even she is unaware of her status. It is imperative she not find out either. Do you understand?"

Franken didn't have a clue what to say. After a short pause, he asked, "What about Ruiz? How is he involved?"

"That is confidential and on a 'need to know' basis, detective. When the investigation gets further along you will understand."

"Okay. So what is it you want me and my partner to do?"

"Go back to Harrison Ramsey and Bob Walker and tell them that you had no success in finding where Kelly Walker went. However, explain to them that you will continue the investigation and get back with them as soon as you find something out. Assure them that you will not suspend the investigation until you find her. Meanwhile, I will keep your Chief in the loop and he will be giving you and your partner further instructions. I appreciate your cooperation and discretion, George"

"No problem. You can trust me and my partner, Director. I'll see Ramsey and Walker first thing tomorrow and speak with them. Then I'll wait for further instructions."

"Thanks George. Again, your discretion is much appreciated." Then Director Hudson hung up.

Franken was overwhelmed. He went into his study so he wouldn't be disturbed by his wife or kids. He poured himself two fingers of bourbon and then he called Esmar Geil.

"Esmar, you are not going to believe this."

CHAPTER 13

Kelly landed at the Minneapolis/St. Paul International airport at 4:35 PM. As a first class passenger she was one of the first off the plane. She landed at one of the furthest gates from the main terminal. It was just under a mile to the main terminal. She immediately texted Marc from her cell phone. He was in the middle of football practice. He immediately called Kelly.

"Marc, I just landed and am walking towards the main terminal. Can you pick me up on the departure level at the Delta terminal?"

"I can be there in about 45 minutes."

"Good I'll meet you there."

Kelly hung up.

Marc asked his assistant coach to finish the practice. He explained to his assistant that an emergency just came up and he had to go straighten things out.

"Is everything alright? Is it your wife or one of your kids?"

"No, it's a friend of mine who needs my help. I appreciate you finishing up here. I'll see you tomorrow."

Marc got in his car and drove to the airport.

While walking to the main terminal, Kelly called Brad Nickolas. She had his number since he had called her on several occasions. She had several of his numbers in her recent calls on her cell phone. She knew he used multiple burner phones. She started calling each of those numbers. The first two numbers didn't work. She then tried the third number. The phone started to ring. Brad answered the phone.

"Well, Kelly Walker or should I say Ana Bannen or Krista Mills? Where the hell are you?"

"Brad, what the Hell was that episode on the beach last week? You scared the Hell out of me and especially my husband. You knew I didn't have any money with me at that time. Explain to me what you were attempting to do? And wait. So it must have been you who slipped those fake passports in my fanny pack on the beach. Was that you?"

"We'll talk about the episode on the beach and the passports later. First where is Omar's half million dollars? And, by the way, those passports are really good fakes."

"I have the money. I'll give it to you, but I want to meet you alone in a public place. Marc Harper will be with me. I have many questions. I want to know what is really going on. And what do you mean those passports are really good fakes?"

"Patience Kelly, all in good time. So where are you now? What city are you in? And when and where do you expect to meet me? Omar is not happy about his money and your betrayal actions. He thought this would come some time later."

"You're talking in riddles. Why are you trying to confuse me? I need the truth. Promise me that you'll finally be honest and explain this whole scheme to me and Marc. If you do, I can be close enough to meet with you tomorrow. We can meet in the Rosedale shopping mall, in the food court at 3:30 PM. Marc and I will be there. The money will be close by for you to pick up after our straight and honest talk. Does that suit you?"

"Not really. Omar is not going to like this. And it's not the time to explain everything to you right now. Our work is not complete. You'll need to trust me for now. But I need that money."

"If I see Omar or any of his muscle with you, there will be no money. In fact don't even tell Omar about this meeting."

"Kelly you are smart, but you are digging a hole you may not be able to get out of."

"Let me worry about that. See you tomorrow."

Kelly then hung up.

Marc picked up Kelly at the Delta concourse about an hour after they spoke. Marc saw the black leather bag.

"Is that Omar's half million dollars?"

"Take me to my house. I can't believe that was your first question you asked me."

"Kelly, you know I care for you. But we both have families. Omar is a dangerous man. I hate what is happening, but we are where we are and we need to finish the job."

"What job? What do you know that I don't?"

"It's was just an expression. I don't know anything more than you. Do you want me to stop and get some fast food on the way to your house?"

"Just like you, change the subject. Sure, get us some food, why not. We have lots to talk about before tomorrow afternoon."

"What's tomorrow?"

"You and I are meeting Brad Nickolas at the Rosedale mall in the food court at 3:00 PM."

"Are you sure that's a good idea?" Omar is going to find out and who knows where it all goes from there."

"Be a man Marc. Something strange is happening. I know you know somethings I don't. I need to know those things. We'll stay up all night if we have to until I figure this out. Now there is a Burger King ahead. Get me a Junior Whopper and fries with a diet Coke."

Marc knew to stop talking. He went through the drive through and got food for the two of them and drove to Kelly's house. Kelly had her garage door opener in the black leather bag. Her husband's car was at the airport long term parking lot. Marc drove his car into the garage next to Kelly's car. He wasn't quite sure what was going to happen from there.

Then Marc said his first words since buying the fast food. "I need to call my wife. She was suspicious when you called late last night. She'll be more suspicious if I don't come home after football practice. How long do you expect for me to be here?"

"As long as it takes. Tell her whatever you want. This is too important. You're welcome to stay the night if you want."

"You know I want to. But I am not sure what to tell my wife. I'll also have to call my school and let them know I won't be there tomorrow."

"Whatever, I am going in the kitchen to eat my Whopper. After you make your calls come and join me."

Marc was having a hard time reading Kelly. Usually they got along famously, but things seemed different this time. So Marc called his school first. That was the easiest call. Then he called his wife. That was a tough one. He told her that he was at 'Little Mogadishu'. Several of his friends, who his wife knew well, were in trouble and they needed his help with the local police and the powers that be at their Mosque. He said he would be home before breakfast. His wife didn't believe a word he said. She told him he needed some confirmation of whatever was happening before he would be welcome back home. She could tell it was another woman. She had felt that Marc had feelings for Kelly Walker, but she thought that was over. She just needed confirmation. Then she hung up. Marc had a bad feeling in his stomach. This was going to be a long night.

The day after Johm Ruiz was cremated his celebration of life was happening in a small ballroom at the downtown Radisson Hotel. Natasha Ruiz was footing the entire bill. There were abundant hors d'oeuvres and an open bar. Alle and Kaydra made up several memory boards of pictures of Johm through his life. Alle and Kaydra both gave heartwarming eulogies for Johm. Natasha was not allowed to speak. That was the agreement amongst the three of them. Over 100 people showed up for the event. Every one of Johm's fellow employees, who weren't at the airport or other ports of entry for customs working, were in attendance. Dr. Fingal was also there. Johm was a well-liked and admired person on the Island.

While that event was happening, Chief Peterson, who unfortunately was unable to attend Johm's celebration of life, was in his office reviewing and confirming the credentials of Dr. Burton Woodcock. The Chief was quite impressed with his credentials. Yale undergraduate, Harvard medical school, Johns Hopkins internship and residency and now chief thoracic surgeon at the Hennepin County Medical Center in Minneapolis. He was and still is a consultant for the Minneapolis FBI and has been for over 10 years.

The Chief called Director Miles Hudson, the director for the Miami FBI office. He asked for a contact for the Minneapolis FBI office to further confirm the doctor's credentials.

"Biob, you can call one of two special agents in Minneapolis for your confirmation. Either Ted Taylor or Darius Clarke," said Hudson, who then gave the Chief both their numbers. "However, I can also vouch for Dr. Woodcock. He has done consulting work for the Miami FBI on several occasions. He is a fine person and even a better doctor. Why do you need confirmation of Dr. Woodcock?"

Chief Peterson then explained how Dr. Woodcock showed up at the funeral home prior to one of the Island's custom agent's cremation and requested a second opinion as to the autopsy of the agent. He explained that no one from the deceased family asked for a second opinion. It was very strange to everyone that an unknown doctor, from Minneapolis, would just show up, unannounced, to perform a second opinion on the autopsy originally performed by the Island's coroner.

"Well, I don't have any idea why Dr. Woodcock would show up like that unless someone from Aruba contacted the FBI in Minneapolis and asked for someone to send another doctor. The FBI must have believed that the person who contacted them had a valid reason to send Dr. Woodcock. He is their best consulting doctor. Why don't you call Ted or Darius?"

"Come to think of it, Alle Thiel, the deceased's girlfriend and fiancé, I think, was the person who insisted she contacted the doctor to perform a second opinion."

"Well, there you go. That's your starting point when you speak with the Minneapolis office."

"Thanks Miles. Hope to meet you some day."

"I hope so too. I need a relaxing vacation."

Chief Peterson then called the Minneapolis office of the FBI.

"May I speak with Special Agent Ted Taylor or Darius Clarke please? This is Chief of Police Biob Peterson for the Island Country of Aruba. I am calling on a case that they may be involved in."

"Please hold Chief, I will attempt to locate one of them," answered the receptionist for the office.

After a hold of about 5 minutes the Chief heard a click on the other end of the phone.

"This is Special Agent Ted Taylor, what can I do for you Chief Peterson?"

The Chief then preceded to explain to the Special Agent the long and somewhat strange story of the death of Johm Ruiz up to the appearance of Dr. Burton Woodcock at the funeral home just before the cremation of Mr. Ruiz.

"I was actually expecting your call Chief. I have just spoken to Dr. Woodcock. He didn't give me the entire background of Mr. Ruiz's death as you have, but, he was sent by this office to Aruba for the purpose of a second opinion on Mr. Ruiz's cause of death."

"May I ask who requested your office to send the doctor?"

"It was a reliable confidential informant who lives in the Minneapolis area. We are working on a very large case of illegal gambling, sex trafficking, extortion, and money laundering."

"How is Aruba and Johm Ruiz involved?" asked the Chief who was very shocked.

"We believe some of the money may be laundered through Aruba. That is all I can tell you at this point. I don't know anything about this Johm Ruiz. As far as I know he isn't involved in the illegal operation. However, he may have found out something since he does work for Aruba customs. But I am not certain. My CI believes he may have found something out about the operation and may have been murdered for that knowledge. Hence, Dr. Woodcock's appearance on the Island. I probably should have contacted you about the second opinion but until we had more information about where the money was actually being laundered we let things play out. I understand that my doctor didn't have a chance to do a second autopsy."

"That's correct, the family wanted his remains cremated right away and refused the second autopsy. However, I did agree to have Dr. Woodcock review our Island coroner's autopsy report and the toxicology report. That is if his credentials were legitimate and for a legitimate purpose. I guess I can now have Dr. Woodcock review our coroner's reports."

"Thank you Chief, I really appreciate that. This is really a very large and complicated case. It's been going on for years. I did hope that Woodcock could have performed an autopsy, but we'll take what we can. I'll update you after our doctor has given me his report."

Special Agent Taylor then hung up. Chief Peterson felt like a fool. He should have called the FBI before the cremation just to make sure his decision was correct. But the family's wishes usually came first.

CHAPTER 14

After Chief Peterson's conversation with Special Agent Taylor of the Minneapolis FBI, he went to the coroner's office to put together Dr. Fingal's autopsy and toxicology reports on Johm Ruiz to give to Dr. Woodcock. He went through all of the coroner's files but couldn't locate either one. He then went to the refrigerated cabinet to obtain Ruiz's autopsy blood and tissue samples that were forwarded to the Carraco lab. Those were also missing. That seemed very strange. Dr. Fingal was a meticulous doctor. He did everything by the book. The Chief thought that maybe Fingal had reviewed all of the paper work at the hospital and took the blood and tissue samples with him.

So the Chief asked his administrative assistant to call Dr. Fingal immediately, at the hospital, and ask him to bring the reports and samples back to the coroner's office.

The assistant had Dr. Fingal's cell phone number since, as the current Island Coroner, he was on 24 hour call. The cell phone rang several times before the doctor answered.

"Who is this calling? I am at Johm Ruiz's celebration of life. And how did you get this number?"

"Doctor, this is Chief Peterson's assistant. I am sorry to bother you but the Chief asked me to call you immediately."

"Don't tell me there is another body to examine. Hasn't this Island had enough drama this month?"

"No sir, it's nothing like that. The Chief wants you to bring John Ruiz's autopsy and toxicology report, along with all of his blood and tissue samples, back to your office at the station. There is another doctor here from the States that needs to review them."

"What are you talking about? What other doctor? I thought this matter was closed."

"I don't know anything about that doctor. I am just following the Chief's orders. When can we expect you to bring those items back?"

There was a long pause. Fingal was confused. What other doctor would need to view those items? After Ruiz's cremation, Fingal shredded his autopsy and fake toxicology reports. All of the samples that were never sent to Curacao were also destroyed along with his dictation. Why would anyone ever care about them again? Fingal, after some thought, then said, "Let me speak with the Chief."

The assistant patched him through to Chief Peterson. "Hello Doctor, what's the problem?"

"Biob, what the Hell is going on? Is there some doctor questioning my work?"

"Jan, no one is questioning your work. I am sure everything you did was accurate. I can't tell you everything, but the FBI has requested one of their consultants to review your findings. It's just a routine matter. Nothing to worry about. If you could just bring all of the reports and samples back to your office I can have the consultant review everything and then he can go back to the States. Just let me know when you can be here so I can call the consultant and have him come to your office."

"Biob, I am at Johm's celebration of life. And then I have a surgery set for this evening," lied Fingal.

"I understand. Just bring them by 10:00 tomorrow morning. I'll have the consultant here at 10:30. See you tomorrow."

Chief Peterson then hung up.

Fingal started to panic. Why in the world would the United States FBI be interested in Ruiz's death? Fingal wasn't even sure of the real cause of death. But during the autopsy it looked like a routine natural cause of death. The cancelation of the $100,000.00 debt to the Marriot casino for an ordinary routine death by natural cause was an easy fix to get Fingal back even on his outstanding gambling debt. Now it may be coming back to haunt him. Even his dictation during his autopsy had been destroyed. What was he going to do? How was he going to explain this to the Chief?

Fingal could only think of one thing. He needed to talk to Harrison Ramsey. He was the one who caused all of this. He had just seen Harrison at the celebration of life. Fingal needed to know why Ramsey wanted everything dealing with Ruiz's death faked. He went back into the celebration. He looked everywhere, but he couldn't find Harrison. Maybe he went back to the hotel?

Fingal picked up the phone and called the Marriott Hotel and asked for Harrison. He told the receptionist that he was a doctor and this was an emergency.

"I just saw Mr. Ramsey go into his office," said the receptionist at the check in counter. "I'll patch you through doctor."

"Hello this is Harrison Ramsey. To whom am I speaking?"

"This is Jan Fingal you asshole. What the Hell really happened to Johm Ruiz? You told me that faking the autopsy and toxicology reports would never be questioned. Your ass is on the hook just as much as mine. So tell me the truth."

"Slow down Fingal. What is going on? I heard that Ruiz's daughter had his body cremated. You and I were even at his celebration of life together. So what's the problem?"

"The problem! This is more than just a problem. This is our freedom."

"Again, what the Hell are you talking about?"

"I just got a call from Chief Peterson. There is some doctor from one of the States FBI offices here as their consultant. He wants to review my autopsy and toxicology report along with all of the blood and tissue samples for Ruiz."

"FBI consultant? Are you sure you heard the Chief correctly?" asked Harrison who thought that he may know something about that.

"Oh he was very clear. He wants all of it tomorrow morning at 10:00 AM. The consultant will review it then. Is that clear enough?"

"I don't understand the problem Fingal. Our deal is still good. Your debt has been taken off the casino's books so no one will ever know it was there. Just give him your reports and the samples. There is no way this consultant would question your results. Your reputation is spotless on the Island. Just calm down."

"I don't think you understand. I wanted to keep that spotless reputation. So after the cremation, I shredded the reports and destroyed all of the samples including my autopsy dictation. There is nothing to give the FBI."

"You got to be kidding. What in the world would make you do such a stupid thing?"

"That train has left the station asshole. The only thing to do is for me is to confess or get off this Island and disappear. If I confess your name will be front and center. The Hell with my gambling debts. You explain to the FBI what happened to Ruiz. You're the only person who really knows."

Harrison then started to panic slightly. He had no idea why Ruiz died. He just thought he was helping one of his co-conspirators in the scheme. He wasn't even sure which one, if any. What a mess.

"Fingal do whatever you have to. It was your autopsy. I'll deny everything. I have made sure that there is no trace of your gambling debt. My casino employees are sworn to secrecy about people who come into the casino. Their jobs are on the line. This is on you and your addiction. You explain it."

Harrison then hung up. He was confused. First Kelly Walker disappeared, now Fingal royally screwed up. The only thing he could think of was to call Brad Nickolas. He had to know something. Maybe that could help him explain his actions away if the FBI came to question him. Then his phone bleeped. It was a text from Kelly.

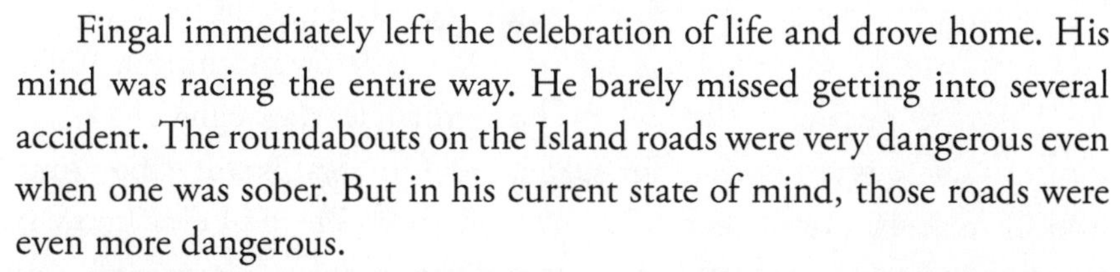

Fingal immediately left the celebration of life and drove home. His mind was racing the entire way. He barely missed getting into several accident. The roundabouts on the Island roads were very dangerous even when one was sober. But in his current state of mind, those roads were even more dangerous.

What was he going to do? What was he going to tell the Chief or the FBI? When he arrived at his home he drove into his garage and the car bumped the garage door as he pushed his garage door opener and the door was opening. He walked into his home as if he was intoxicated. His wife noticed his actions and asked him what was wrong. She wanted to know if something happened at the hospital. Did one of his patients die? Fingal ignored her, said nothing and walked into his study.

He closed the door and locked it. He sat at his desk and opened the top drawer. He took out a bottle of 14 year old scotch and a crystal rocks glass. He poured several ounces into the glass. He took several gulps until all of the liquor was gone. Then he poured some more. Now what? His wife was knocking on his door and begging him to come out.

"Tell me what's wrong, Jan. I have never seen you like this. Have you been gambling again? I know about your gambling. It's alright we can sort this out. Just open the door. You're scaring me."

"Go away, leave me alone. Everything is okay. I just need some time to myself. I can work this out. It has nothing to do with any gambling or you. This is an issue I have to work out."

His wife didn't know what to do. She knew he had gone to Johm Ruiz's celebration of life. Maybe he went to the hospital after that? Maybe she should call the hospital and speak with one of the doctors to see what happened. Fingal finished his second glass of scotch. He then took out his keys from his pocket and unlocked the bottom drawer of his desk. He took out a false bottom from that drawer. He was in a daze. He felt around until he touched it. He then removed it. It was his Glock 17 and one of its clips. He had no idea how many rounds, if any, were in the clip. He cocked the semi-automatic weapon. He held it in his hand for several moments just staring at it. His hands were perspiring. He poured some more scotch into his glass with his free hand. He took another sip of the scotch. Then he put the barrel of the Glock into his mouth, closed his eyes, and pulled the trigger. The sound could be heard several houses away.

His wife screamed. She fell to the floor. "Jan, Jan open the door. Please." There was nothing but silence. Off in the distance she heard sirens. Then she blacked out.

When she woke up she was on a paramedic gurney being transported to an ambulance. She could see another gurney but couldn't make out who it was on it. On the way to the hospital she took off the oxygen mask and asked the paramedic about her husband. He put the mask back over her mouth and told her that he was very sorry for her loss. She blacked out again.

Chief Peterson got a call 10 minutes after the police broke open Fingal's study door. One of the police officers was a rookie. He looked at the scene, went outside the home and vomited. The rookie's partner told the Chief that he needed to appoint a new Island coroner and send a hearse to the Fingal home.

The Chief asked what the Hell happened. Did his officer have any idea who shot Fingal? The officer explained the situation and Chief Peterson fell back into his chair and almost started to cry. Then he asked about the doctor's wife. He wanted to know if she was all right. He was told that she was not hurt but was on the way to the Island's main hospital. Why would Jan take his own life? The Chief had to find out. This incident was just off the chart.

The Chief immediately got into his car and drove to the emergency room. It was the longest ride of his life. How could he console her? What questions would he ask her? What could have triggered all these eccentric events over the last few days? There had been too many incidents happening for all of this to be just a minor event happening in Aruba. Chief Peterson's first call, from his car, was to Special agent Ted Taylor in Minneapolis. The Chief was not going to hang up until he was informed as to what was precisely happening.

CHAPTER 15

Kelly and Marc were at Kelly's home sitting in her family room. Marc had just finished speaking with his wife on the phone. Kelly had finished her Burger King meal in about 10 minutes. Marc had not touched any of his food.

"Aren't you going to eat your burger and fries?" asked Kelly.

"Kelly, I just got off the phone with my wife and I lied to her about where I am and what I am doing. I could tell she knew I was lying. I feel terrible. You and I have always been good friends. Maybe even more than friends at times. But everything that is happening right now is just eating me up inside."

"What are talking about?"

"I am so sorry that I got you and Bob involved with Omar in this entire 'Little Mogadishu' scheme. I really love my wife and kids and even my teaching job. Except for this scheme, I like the way my life turned out. I wish I could turn back the clock, but I know that's impossible. This scheme is starting to scare me and make me sick. Omar scares me. Now you are even scaring me."

"Let me take you off the hook, Marc," started Kelly as she took Marc's burger and took a bite. "You and I could have been a couple years ago. I even remember you and me discussing whether we should become a couple or I should marry Bob. You were the one who encouraged me to marry Bob and take that job in Utah. Trust me when I tell you that was the best thing I could have done. I like you a lot. In some uncanny way I even love you. But romantically you and I are never going to be a couple. However, we will always be very good friends forever. Unless you can tell me what we are really accomplishing working with Omar and Brad and, more importantly, exactly what their end game is for this scheme, then you should go home to your wife, make love and tell her you deeply love her.

Neither Harrison, Bob nor I understand why we are involved in this scheme, other than making a few bucks by facilitating the transfer of a lot of money from off shore accounts to other off shore accounts. And we don't even do much of that. Brad does the vast majority of it. It's Omar that's making a fortune and we are taking a huge risk so he can get rich."

"Kelly, thank you for understanding. I agree. I feel better. You're the smartest one of all of us involved in this crazy scheme. However, by disappearing like you did with all that money, I just hope you know what you're doing. But I will follow through with whatever plan you have."

"Thank you Marc. I think we cleared up a lot in just a couple of minutes. Now, meet me at the Rosedale food court at 2:30 tomorrow afternoon. Brad is meeting us there at 3:00. I am going to press him hard on what is really happening. I feel, deep in my bones, that something other than what we are told is happening is really going on. I will not give Brad Nickolas any money until he tells us what that is. I know we may be taking a risk, but we can always work it out with Brad if my intuition is wrong. I'll just give him the money. Are you with me?"

"Damn right I am."

"Then get the Hell out of here and give your wife a kiss for me. See you tomorrow."

Marc gave Kelly a kiss on her cheek and left to go home. Kelly finished Marc's burger and fries and got ready to go to bed. She knew that she needed to communicate something to her husband and Harrison to let them know that she was all right. However, she didn't want to tell them about the next day's meeting or where she was sleeping that night. So Kelly took out her cell phone and texted Harrison and Bob:

'Guys, I am okay and in a safe place. The money I took is also safe. I will call you both soon to let you know where I am and explain everything to you. Meanwhile, please trust me. Love you both.'

The morning after Jan Fingal killed himself, Dr. Woodcock showed up at the police station at 10:30. Fingal's body was resting in one of the four refrigerated drawers located in the coroner's office. An autopsy was required to be performed, under Aruba law. However, Chief Peterson first needed to appoint a new coroner for the Island.

"Chief, you look like you haven't slept in a week. What's going on?" asked Dr. Woodcock.

"It was a long and eventful night. And I have some bad news for you doctor."

"I guess you'll need to explain that to me."

"Last night, Dr. Jan Fingal, the Island's coroner who supposedly did the autopsy on Johm Ruiz, committed suicide."

"What do you mean supposedly did the autopsy? And why, in God's name, would he kill himself?"

"I have no idea. His wife is still in the emergency room sedated. I tried to speak with her last night but she was unable to communicate. I will try to speak with her, hopefully, later today. My officers searched his home office and the rest of his home to attempt to locate the autopsy and toxicology report for Johm Ruiz, as well as the samples sent to the Carraco lab. They were nowhere to be found. Fingal was aware that all of those items were to be kept strictly in the morgue in certain designated secure files and refrigerated areas."

"So what I hear your saying is that Fingal either didn't actually perform an autopsy on Ruiz or all of the records are nowhere to be found. And that begs the question about the correctness of Ruiz's death certificate."

Just as Dr. Woodcock was in the middle of speaking, Chief Peterson's assistant came into his office and handed him a note. He had instructed his assistant to contact the Curacao lab and get a copy of the toxicology report. The Chief read the note and then handed it to Woodcock. The doctor read it to himself and then looked up at the Chief.

"Is this really possible? The Curacao lab indicates that they never received any blood or tissue samples or other request from the Aruba coroner, in at least, the last 12 months to determine toxicology results for anyone, including a Johm Ruiz. What kind of nonsensical policing office are you running here Chief?"

"I resent those comments doctor. I skimmed Dr. Fingal's autopsy and toxicology report. I saw Fingal sign Ruiz's death certificate. It was Fingal's responsibility to file those reports in the proper locations. I don't follow every employ, especially one who doesn't even get paid, everywhere they may go to make sure they do their jobs. I hire people I trust to do their job. Dr. Fingal had always been a trustworthy person, physician and coroner. I have no idea what happened in this case. But I will have this matter investigated. Maybe we just haven't looked in every one of the locations he may have left the reports before he was to file them here."

"I find it a strange coincident that less than 24 hours after I arrived on the Island to perform a second opinion autopsy on John Ruiz the coroner who performed the original autopsy commits suicide. What do you think Chief?"

"I'll tell you what I think after my detectives do their work."

Dr. Woodcock patted Chief Peterson on his shoulder and sat in one of the Chief's desk chairs. He looked the Chief directly in the eyes and said, "Look Chief, I am not accusing you, or any of your officers, of any wrong doing. Everything I hear about the law enforcement community on this Island has been good. But in this particular matter, you have been placed in a bad situation. I understand. I will call my contact at the Minneapolis FBI, Ted Taylor, and explain to him the situation. I will take my instructions from him. I'm fairly certain he will want me back home until this matter is resolved. I am truly sorry Chief. I wish you good luck in your investigation."

With that comment the two men shook hands and Dr. Woodcock left the building to go back to his hotel. Chief Peterson called detective George Franken and instructed him and his partner to investigate Dr. Fingal's alleged suicide. He wanted a full report on every aspect of Fingal's life that could have caused this tragedy. He told him to interview his wife, co-workers and locations that he frequented. The Chief even mentioned that there was a rumor that Fingal may have had a gambling issue. There were dozens of casinos on the Island. He wanted each manager of those casinos interviewed. Franken and Geil just couldn't understand all of the strange occurrences that have happened in such a short period of time. They knew that they had their work cut out for them.

After the Chief's call, Franken and Geil went to the emergency room at Aruba's main hospital. Dr. Fingal was the chief of thoracic surgery at that hospital. Both detectives knew that his wife would be well cared for. She was finally coming to the reality that her beloved husband had killed himself. In some bizarre way, she believed the suicide was her fault. She knew about his gambling difficulties. She should have insisted on her husband getting psychiatric help or at least insisted on him joining gamblers anonymous. With so many casinos on the Island there were several assemblies for people who needed help with gambling addictions.

She managed his finances as well as the household finances. She knew how much he lost when he was gambling. She confronted him several times, but never followed up. Most likely, because their finances were not that bad. So either the doctor owed a lot of money to bookies and casinos that she didn't know about or maybe, she hoped, he was a lucky gambler. However she now felt it must have been the former.

"Mrs. Fingal, my name is George Franken and this is my partner, Esmar Geil. We are so sorry for your loss. Your husband was not only an excellent physician but a true gentleman. We worked with him a few times on a few mortalities over the last few years. Thankfully, none of which were criminal. But, as the coroner, he was always available to give his time for this wonderful Island."

"You're too kind. I appreciate that. Jan was a hard worker and a good man. I just don't know what I'll do without him. I don't even believe that I can return to that house. And now I have to arrange a funeral."

"I am sure that the administration of this hospital will make sure that you are well taken care of and will get all the help you need. Everyone here loved your husband," said Franken. "Do you feel up to a few questions?"

"Of course. I understand that you have a job to do."

"Could you tell us exactly what happened starting when your husband arrived at your home last night?"

She was able to elaborate on his physical condition starting when the top of his car hit the garage door as he was pulling into the garage; his demeanor; his inability to answer her questions; and locking himself in his study. She continued until she heard a gunshot. The she started to cry.

"Do you need some time?"

"No, I want to get this over with. Please continue," as she was drying her eyes.

"Do you know if your husband may have had a location in your home or some other place where he would have stored police documents or a refrigeration unit where he would keep samples of blood or tissue for his work as the coroner?"

"No. Jan always kept his government work at the police station. He never took anything concerning the coroner work home. He was meticulous about that. There wasn't even a refrigerator in the home for those types of things. We have a wine cooler and our kitchen refrigerator. We don't have a second refrigerator. Whenever he was able to come home early from work we would always go out to eat. I did all the shopping so I always knew what was in the fridge," Mrs. Fingal was somewhat confused. "Why are you asking me about his coroner's work? Shouldn't your questions be about our finances and his gambling? Isn't that why he..." She couldn't finish the sentence and she began to cry again.

Franken and Geil looked at each other. They were thankful that Mrs. Fingal brought up the gambling issue. They weren't quite sure how to start that conversation. She was very open about the doctor's gambling issues, but she was certain that he wouldn't have committed suicide over his compulsion.

She was even willing to give the detectives all of their finances. That would show that he really hadn't lost that much. Their finances were normal for their income. Although she did mention that maybe he had obtained a line of credit at some casino or with a bookie and maybe he was overdrawn on that. Maybe someone was threatening him about that. But she had no idea where or who that may be. But no matter how much he may have owed, I know that he wouldn't have killed himself over a few dollars. She was as cooperative as she could.

The detectives asked a few more questions about their daily lives. Has anyone threatened her or her husband? Did anyone have a grudge against him? Was there a patient who may have had a bad result? She didn't know anything concerning those matters. The detectives thanked her and wished her well. They felt rotten about their questions and her circumstances.

The Chief wanted to know about Ruiz's autopsy reports. Franken and Geil got nothing from the wife. Why would he kill himself? Was it his gambling? It didn't sound like it. Was he having an affair? They didn't believe that either. It had to do with something about Ruiz. But What? So the detectives decided to go next to the Marriott Hotel. They were told by the FBI to speak with Harrison and Bob about the update on Kelly's disappearance. Also the Marriott Hotel had the largest casino on the Island. There was a large area for the high rollers. Maybe Harrison could shed some light on Fingal's gambling.

CHAPTER 16

At 2:30 PM, the afternoon after Kelly arrived in Minneapolis she entered the North entrance of the Rosedale Mall with the black leather bag holding half million dollars in it. She first went to the lockers located at that entrance, put four quarters into locker number 45, turned the key and opened the locker. She placed the black leather bag into the locker and closed the door and took the key and placed it in her purse.

Kelly then went to the directory for the mall located at the North entrance. She located where the food court was situated. She went directly there, ordered two Caribou ice coffees and sat at a table for 4. Several minutes later Marc walked into the food court. He found Kelly and sat down.

"I bought you an ice coffee."

"Will you tell me exactly what we're going to be doing here?

"Do you trust me, my good friend?

"Of course I do."

"I trust you a lot, Marc," as she pulled the locker key out of her purse. "Here is a key. Put it in your pocket and do not lose it. Do not tell Brad you have it. Unless I ask you for it, keep it secure somewhere at your home. Don't tell your wife or anyone else you have it. Do you understand?"

"No, but I trust you."

"Let me do the talking. No matter how mad I may get, please don't try to intervene. Do what I ask of you and don't ask any questions. If you do that we'll get through this. But most important, we'll find out what the end game is on this scheme."

Marc nodded approval of Kelly's questionable plan as Brad Nickolas sat down at the table.

"Kelly. Marc. Nice to see you."

The three of them stared at each other for a minute. Then Brad broke the silence.

"No coffee for me?"

"What would you like?" Kelly asked.

"A small ice coffee, two sugars and a little cream."

"Marc, would you get our friend some ice coffee?" said Kelly.

As Marc got up to get in line at the Caribou coffee kiosk, Brad said to Kelly, "Where's the money? That's why I'm here. The only reason I'm here."

"First, I want to know why I'm here. We have been transporting money from Minneapolis to Aruba for the sole purpose of giving it to you or one of your patsies. You, or someone else, unknown to me or my husband or friends, fixes it so that we are never searched when we go through US or Aruba customs. Then you transfer the money somewhere else in the Caribbean. Diric Omar directs the whole operation. My husband and I get $1000.00 each every week of the year put in a numbered account in an Aruba bank. I'm not sure what Harrison and Marc get. And I don't even know how Marc gets his money since he has never been to Aruba. Bob and I can take out our money whenever we please. We have been doing this favor for Omar for several years, illegally and without our consent, all based on some vague threat of injury to one of us or our families if we didn't comply. Aruba reports any local bank accounts of US citizens to the US. Even private banks. The IRS probably knows we have money offshore but yet they have never contacted any of us about it. We don't declare it as income. We don't receive any Aruba Department of Revenue forms. Harrison and I have heard about many threats of injury by Omar and you, but yet we are unaware of anyone hurt, as far as we know. Even if we were late or screwed up on a deposit or giving you money, nothing has really happened. I have two fake passports passed to me. I believe you gave them to me. You wanted me to disappear without the police finding out. What the Hell is going on? What are my husband and my friends involved in? What's Omar's end game? When do we stop? And what happens to us when it all stops? Nothing adds up."

While Kelly is asking all her questions, Marc comes back to the table and hands Brad his iced coffee and sits down.

"Thanks Marc."

"What did I miss?" asked Marc.

"Kelly has been making some allegations and asking me some questions. Do you have any more questions Kelly?"

"What happened to Johm Ruiz? Why was he murdered? He had to be one of Omar's people. He began processing Bob and I when we went through customs. Who murdered him? Did Ruiz threaten to go to the police? One of Omar's patsies was murdered. Now, out of the blue, this has become frightening. I need to know the truth."

"Are you through?" asked Brad.

"I told you Brad, answer my questions and explain this scheme to me and you'll get the money."

Marc said nothing but started to get a little nervous.

"I told you on the phone that you and your friends need to be patient. You will find out everything and all your questions will be answered in due time. But right now I need that money. I'm not leaving without it. Where is it?"

"I have it. It's close by. Just answer my questions."

Brad looked at Marc and asked him, "Where is the money?"

Marc said nothing.

"If you know where the money is tell me. If you don't know where the money is then leave now."

Marc looked at Kelly. She said to Marc, "Tell him the truth."

"I have no idea where the money is."

"Then get out of here now. This is between Kelly and me," said Brad with a tone that scared Marc.

Marc looked at Kelly. She said to Marc, "Please leave. Brad and I will work this out. I'll call you later."

"No, I'm staying. I'm as much a part of this as you are Kelly."

"No, please leave. We talked about this. I'll call you."

Marc bitterly got up and walked out of the mall. He felt like he had just forsaken his best friend. But he knew Kelly could handle herself. He drove home to his wife and went into his home as if he was coming home from his teaching job. He kissed his wife like nothing happened. Then he reached into his pocket and felt the key.

"Okay Kelly. Last chance. Where is the money? Said Brad in a very threatening manner. "If you don't give me the right answer, your husband will not know where you are. I just spoke with Harrison. Your husband just left Aruba and is on his way back to St. Paul. He will have no idea where you are when he walks into your home unless you give me the money. He knows about you flying to Miami on a false passport. He'll figure out that you somehow made it to St. Paul with the money. The Aruba police force were a lot savvier than I thought."

"Do what you have to do. No answers, no money."

"Okay get up and turn around and put your hands behind you."

"What are you talking about?"

"You're under arrest. You will sit in a Federal holding cell until I get the money."

Kelly didn't understand, but by sheer instinct she stood up and put her hands behind her back just to see what would happen. Brad put handcuffs on her but did not recite her Miranda rights. He then escorted her to his car.

"You're a cop?" said Kelly nearly speechless.

"FBI. Special agent Bradley Carr of the Minneapolis division of organized crime. You should have just cooperated like you and your friends have been doing. You could have been home in your nice comfortable bed tonight. And two more things. First, nobody murdered anyone. We have no idea what happened to John Ruiz. I was hoping that maybe you or your friends Harrison Ramsey or Marc Harper could elaborate on that matter. We'll have someone contact them about Ruiz. Second, you're right, I had those passports made up and passed them to you. I knew you would take advantage and run. I just didn't think you would take the money. You were starting to figure things out and your curiosity would bring you to me. I didn't want you discussing the scheme with the others. It was too important for the FBI to see this through."

Kelly was now totally confused. She thought about telling Brad about the money. But she knew he wouldn't tell her about the scheme. So she decided not to contest the arrest. Somehow she would figure out how to get in touch with her husband and the others to let them know about the FBI. However, she had over thought her current predicament and didn't quite understand how naïve she really was.

Under Chief Peterson's orders, Detectives Franken and Geil drove to the Marriott Hotel to speak with Harrison Ramsey about Dr. Fingal's suicide. When they arrived at the hotel they went to the check in desk to ask for Ramsey. The clerk told the detectives that Harrison had just finished for the day and was having a drink with a friend at the lobby bar. As they walked towards the bar, they saw Ramsey sitting at a high top table with a woman who they thought looked familiar but where unsure of her name. Ramsey had a short rocks glass and the woman was drinking a martini. The detectives spoke to each other about interrupting them and decided that the woman must either be Harrison's girlfriend or they may be discussing something about Kelly's disappearance, but they just were not quite sure. So they decided to wait a few minutes to see if the woman would leave after her drink.

Harrison was having a drink with Alle Thiel. She had returned to speak with Harrison after Brad Nickolas had required her to find out about the whereabouts of Kelly and to allow Dr. Woodcock to perform a second autopsy on Johm Ruiz. She was explaining to Harrison that she had failed on both those demands. She was terrified at the consequences and she was enlisting his help on what to tell Brad.

Harrison had no answer to the whereabouts of Kelly and was aware that Dr. Woodcock didn't perform the second autopsy. Kaydra insisted, with Chief Peterson's consent, to have her father's body cremated.

"I finally convinced Kaydra to go back to Gainesville and finish her studies. There was nothing more she could do for her father anymore. She agreed and flew back to Florida," said Alle to Harrison.

"Did her father have any insurance or other benefits to help her out?" asked Harrison.

"He has a $100,000.00 insurance policy through work. His house, car and personal property will be sold so she will have sufficient additional funds to get her through school. She is a great kid and deserves a good life. I will help her out with the legal issues on the Island. We have become good friends."

"Does she know anything about you and Omar?"

"No, and I want to leave it that way."

During their discussion, Harrison called his server over and ordered another drink for the two of them. That was when the detectives decided to approach them.

"Harrison Ramsey, do you remember us, detective George Franken and my partner Esmar Geil?"

"Of course, but can't this wait for another time. Ms. Thiel and I are having drinks."

"Alle Thiel? asked Franken. "You were Johm Ruiz's fiancé. You were the person who requested Dr. Burton Woodcock to come to Aruba, from the United States, to perform a second autopsy on Ruiz. Correct?"

"No, I was only Johm's good friend, not his fiancé. And yes, I did request a second autopsy, but what does that have to do with the Aruba police?"

"Well, we have several matters to discuss with both of you about Kelly Walker's disappearance and Johm Ruiz's death. So I think you should make this a good time to talk. We drove all the way out here to give you some information, Harrison. But, to have Ms. Thiel here saves us another trip."

Both Harrison and Alle looked at each other and were somewhat confused. After all, Harrison had just met Alle a day ago. However, they both nodded to the detectives and agreed to listen to them.

Detective Franken started by saying, "Harrison we have an update on Kelly Walker. It seems that she had at least one or maybe even more fake passports. And for reasons we are still unsure of, she decided to leave Aruba with something very valuable in that black leather bag you saw her with on the security tapes. We thought that maybe you or her husband may have some knowledge of what was in the bag."

"Okay wait a minute. There is no way that I have any idea what was in that bag," lied Harrison. "Also, Kelly Walker is not the type of person who would know anyone who could obtain fake passports. She is just a regular tourist who loves Aruba and a good friend of mine. I know her well. Trust me."

"Well it seems that your good friend walked to the Hyatt hotel, purchased some clothes and sundries, took a cab to the airport and purchased a one way ticket to Miami under the name of Krista Mills. Here is a picture of her with her fake passport going through customs two nights ago," as Franken shows Harrison the passport, ticket and custom's picture.

"I find that preposterous."

"Our office contacted the Miami FBI to find her, but she must have had another fake passport under another name and flew off somewhere else. Do you know where that may be? Or how about her husband? Would he know? And where is he by the way? It's too bad that the US doesn't take pictures of passengers on domestic flights. Otherwise we could have tracked her," said Franken. "Why do you think she wanted out of Aruba with whatever she had in that bag?"

"I find everything you are telling me fascinating, but if what you are telling me is true, then maybe I didn't know Kelly as well as I thought. And by the way, her husband, Bob, flew home to St. Paul yesterday. He was hoping that Kelly would probably attempt to contact him there rather than in Aruba. Trust me he doesn't know anything about fake passports or what's in the bag either."

"Ramsey, we just don't believe you. We may need you to come down to the station, in a day or two after we have completed our investigation, to discuss this all over again. So think hard about what you really know. We will find out a lot. The FBI has now come on board in this investigation."

"What investigation? Kelly's disappearance, which you told me, no crime was committed? Or Johm Ruiz's death was of natural causes? I don't understand. And why would the FBI be interested in those two non-crimes," questioned Harrison.

Franken and Geil looked at Harrison attempting to determine if was telling the truth. Both had a feeling that he was holding something back.

So they told Harrison that they would discuss the death of Johm Ruiz. Alle then put her drink down and became interested. Both detectives noticed that immediately.

"The day that Dr. Woodcock was unable to perform the second autopsy on Ruiz, Chief Peterson promised Woodcock that he would have full access to Dr. Fingal's autopsy report, toxicology report and the samples of the blood and tissue sent to the lab. Woodcock wasn't completely satisfied, but he acknowledged that would have to do."

"So Dr. Woodcock probably came to the same conclusion as Dr. Fingal as to Johm's cause of death, right?" asked Harrison carefully.

"No, he didn't. In fact he didn't come to any conclusion. He just left the Island and went back to Minneapolis where he works at one of their hospitals," said Franken.

"I don't understand," said Alle. "Why didn't he come to any conclusion?"

Harrison looked confused but he knew where they were going. After all Harrison took great risks in making sure Johm Ruiz's autopsy and toxicology report were very clean showing a death by natural causes. It was Fingal who screwed up.

"I guess neither of you have heard about Dr. Fingal," said Geil.

"Heard what?" asked Harrison.

Detective Franken then restated the entire sequence of events leading up to Fingal's suicide including the search for all of the autopsy reports and samples that had disappeared. He then indicated to both Harrison and Alle, who were in shock, that the lack of reports and tissue and blood samples was the reason Woodcock left the Island. Also, he included the fact that it was really the Minneapolis FBI, and not Alle Thiel, who had demanded the second autopsy.

Woodcock worked for the FBI on certain cases, including this one. Alle couldn't believe what she was hearing. She wondered what Brad was up to when he demanded her to make sure there was a second autopsy. Harrison actually felt some relief that Fingal was dead. Now he couldn't implicate him on cancelling his debt with the casino.

After some time for Harrison and Alle to let all of this information sink in, Harrison said, "So what's your conclusions detectives?"

"We believe that Kelly may have had all of Fingal's autopsy reports and tissue samples in that black bag. We also believe that you both knew about that and encouraged her to run. You have been lying to us all the time. Kelly had those fake passports when she came to Aruba each time, just in case there was a reason to use them. We don't know what she and her husband were carrying in and out of the Country, but the FBI thinks there may have been some money laundering going on. We know that Ruiz checked Bob and Kelly in and out of customs every time they came to Aruba. That cannot be a coincidence. So maybe there was some money in that black bag also," insinuated Franken.

"So what are you saying detective?" Asked Harrison.

"You tell me Harrison. Or, how about you Ms. Thiel?"

"I don't know what to say. I am as shocked about all of this concerning Fingal and Kelly. None of it makes any sense to me. This is the first I have heard about any of it," said Harrison.

"I feel the same way," said Alle.

"We'll see," said Franken. "We'll be in touch and let you know when to come to the station for some more questions. We have a few more matters to investigate. Sleep tight. We're on the case."

CHAPTER 17

Bob Walker landed at the Minneapolis/St. Paul International airport at 4:30 PM the day Kelly was locked in a Federal holding cell at the Federal building in downtown Minneapolis. The first thing Bob did, as he was exiting the plane, was to call Kelly from his cell phone. It went to voice mail. That was the fourth time he attempted to call her that day with the same results. He needed to find out what happened to Kelly after she landed in Miami. He had forgot that she left her cell phone in their hotel room.

Even the Aruba detectives could not determine where she went from there. Why did she disappear like that? What was in the black bag? The only other person Bob could call who may have any knowledge of Kelly's whereabouts would be Marc Harper. He always felt that Marc and Kelly had some type of connection, but he never wanted to inquire. He knew Kelly liked him a lot. But, he believed that their marriage was strong. And Marc was not the type of person to cheat on his family. So he called Marc.

Marc thought it would be Kelly. He was anxious to know what happened between Brad and Kelly after he left. Neither called him. That was not like Kelly. She would have usually called after a meeting like that. Also, he wanted to know what to do with the key she gave him. He thought the money Brad wanted was locked somewhere and the key was crucial for finding the money. He hoped Kelly wasn't going to hold the money hostage to get his friends out of the scheme. But he was sure that Kelly had some sort of plan. Then Marc's phone rang.

"Hello," Marc said anxiously thinking it was finally Kelly.

"Hello Marc, this is Bob Walker."

"Bob, it's been a while. Where are you?"

I just landed in Minneapolis. I am on my way to the long term parking lot to pick up my car. I just flew home from Aruba. Do you know if my car will be there when I arrive?"

"What kind of question is that?"

"Did Kelly pick it up? Is she here in town?"

"I am not sure where you're coming from."

"You know that Kelly disappeared from Aruba several days ago don't you?"

"Yes, I heard. She called me two days ago when she landed in Minneapolis. She asked me to pick her up and take her home. I thought she wanted to keep your car at the airport for you when you got back," Marc finally confessed.

"So you saw her?

"Yes, I picked her up and took her home."

"Did she tell you why she disappeared? Did she have a black leather bag with her?

"Bob, I had no idea that Kelly would disappear with all that money. I never asked her why and she didn't tell me."

"How much money are we talking about, Marc?

"You don't know?

"No one told me. Harrison acted like he didn't know either. He was quite concerned when she disappeared. I knew that it must have been a lot of money. I hope Omar and Brad don't find out that she took it or where she is." "Bob, It's over a half million dollars. Brad knows. He is really pissed. Kelly arranged a meeting with Brad and me today at the Rosedale mall. Kelly hid the money somewhere before our meeting. She wanted Brad to explain the entire scheme to her and to find out when it would be over and what his and Omar's end game was. She told him that she wouldn't give Brad the money until she got the answers she wanted."

"Did he give her the answers she wanted?"

"I don't know. I was told to leave the meeting while Brad and Kelly figured it all out."

"So did they figure it out? Asked Bob nervously.

"I don't know. Kelly hasn't called me. I tried to call her several times but it went to voice mail. I tried Brad also, but there was no answer."

"Why in the Hell would you leave Kelly all alone with Brad? He is Omar's right hand man. Who knows what he would do to Kelly to get that money. You are an asshole coward."

"Bob, you don't understand. You weren't there. Kelly believes something concerning this scheme is happening other than having us help Omar launder his money. You know how smart she is. If I didn't leave there when I was told, who knows what would have happened. Go home Bob. She'll probably be there waiting for you."

"Damn it Marc. This scheme has really gotten out of hand. How in the Hell did we get here? Are you sure you have told me everything you know?"

Marc thought about the key and what Bob may do if he knew that Kelly couldn't give Brad the money.

"I have told you everything I know, Bob," Marc lied. "Call me when you get home and let me know if Kelly is there. If I hear from her you'll be the first person I call."

Bob hung up. He was dropped off by the airport shuttle bus next to his car which was parked where he and Kelly left it over a week before. He drove directly home. When he arrived, Kelly's car was not in the garage. The house was empty. There was no black leather bag anywhere in the house. But on Bob's desk in the study was a folded note with Bob's name on the outside. He picked it up and unfolded it. He read it to himself:

'Bob I love you very much. I am so sorry that I must have scared you when I left Aruba like I did. There was something that had been bothering me for some time about Brad and Omar. I needed to find it out for myself. I knew that if I told you or Harrison what I thought neither of you would have believed me. For sure, neither of you would have let me confront Brad or Omar by myself. What I did is on me. No one else made me leave like I did. Forgive me. If you're reading this and I'm not home, call Brad Nickolas on one of his burner phones. He'll know where I am. I have three numbers for him.

612-555-4267, 305-555-2324, 415-555-0829

I love you. I always have.

Kelly'

Bob read the note three times. What has Kelly done? Why does Brad have three burner phones? How did she get the fake passports? Bob imagined what someone would do if half million dollars of theirs was stolen. Bob grabbed his cell phone and called the first number on the list.

After detectives Franken and Geil left the Marriott Hotel, they went back to the downtown police station. On their way there Geil turned to his partner and said, "Why didn't you ask Harrison Ramsey about Fingal's gambling issue. Ramsey would know if Fingal had a line of credit at the casino. I thought that Fingal's gambling debt may have been at least a contributing factor in his suicide?"

"Fingal may have had a gambling issue, but his wife would have emphasized that part of his life a lot more. When we spoke with her she was willing to completely cooperate by giving us all of their financials, bank records, etc. She ran his medical practice. She paid his bills. She paid the house expenses. She knew her husband's income and investments. She even admitted he liked to gamble. But I don't believe that course for this investigation is currently convincing. If nothing else pans out we can go there, but first we should continue investigating Johm Ruiz's death."

"Okay George, but where do we start?"

"We need to find a connection between Ruiz and Fingal. Even a third party connection tying them together. You start writing down possible names that we should investigate who may have a connection, even remotely, between Fingal and Ruiz."

Detective Geil took out his small notebook and started writing down names as he verbalized them to his partner. "Let me start with the obvious. First is Alle Theil. She was Ruiz's girlfriend. We just met her. For all we know she had reason to hurt Ruiz. That may have caused her to want to get rid of the autopsy materials."

"Now you're starting to think like a real detective Esmar. So who's next?"

"Kelly and Bob Walker. Ruiz has been their customs agent for some time. Who knows what Ruiz may have found out about them? Also Irving

Wernet. He was Ruiz's immediate supervisor. He handled the Walker's customs entries and exits before Ruiz."

Geil went on to name 7 more names, including Fingal's wife, who may have had a connection to either Ruiz or Fingal or have a connection between them. Franken was impressed as to how his rookie detective was thinking. But when Geil named Chief Peterson, Franken stopped the car and pulled over.

"You were doing such a good job Esmar. But the Chief? How long have we known him? And how do you figure he has a criminal connection between Fingal and Ruiz?"

"I'm so sorry if I offended you George, but you told me to look at everyone who may be connected, even remotely, to Fingal and Ruiz. The Chief knew them both. He had access to the coroner's office. He also knew Ruiz's ex-wife Natasha. She's on my list."

"Except for knowing Natasha Ruiz, you and I fit into the same category as the Chief. Do you want to add our names?"

"Give me a break Franken. The Chief knows Miles Hudson, head of the Miami FBI. Hudson knows the two Minneapolis FBI agents who were interested in Ruiz's autopsy. In fact didn't the Chief say that it was the FBI who sent Dr. Woodcock for the second autopsy? Maybe, just maybe, the FBI is involved somehow with Ruiz and Fingal."

"Holy crap! You are becoming a damn good detective Geil. I should have thought about that. We really need to look into the FBI angle on all of this. But our Chief. We need to take him off the list."

As the detectives made their way through the streets of Aruba on their way downtown, detective Franken started to think about the FBI connection. Geil may have nailed something. But what? Meantime, Geil was making notes in his notebook and for the first time during this entire unique investigation, Geil felt like a real detective. No more words were spoken between the detectives until they arrived at the downtown station. Franken then said that they should see if the Chief is in. We need to sit down with him and go over the list and the FBI connection. Three heads would be better than two. And the Chief was once a top notch detective himself.

Bob Walker called the first number on Kelly's list. No answer. Then he dialed the second number.

"Yes, who is this?" said Brad Nickolas.

"This is Bob Walker, Brad. Where is my wife?"

"Walker, she is in a safe place. She will remain there until she tells me where the money is. Maybe you know where it is? Do you?"

"What kind of cat and mouse game are you and Omar playing? Kelly and I have been good soldiers for several years. Actually, Kelly has really been your top soldier. You seem to trust her more than even Marc Harper. I don't understand why we can't just all get together. We have worked together for years. Then you can tell me, Marc and Kelly what Omar's and your end game really is. We have to find out sometime"

"Walker you are naïve. You and Marc need to get me that money. One of you knows where it is. Until then, I will not be having any more contact with you, Marc, Harrison or Alle. Until I get the money Omar and I will be working a different angle. So if you want to see your wife, get me the money."

"Who's Alle?" questioned Bob.

Brad hung up.

"Damn it." Yelled Bob as he dialed Marc's number.

Marc saw Bob's name on his cell phone as it rang. He knew Kelly wasn't at their home. And he didn't want to speak with Bob yet. He needed to try to figure this all out himself. If Kelly may have figured it out, maybe he could. Then he could work out a deal with Brad. He had to go over everything that had happened since he got that first call for a favor from Omar. What the Hell was happening? What was the alternative plan that Brad had for him and his friends? And where is Kelly?

CHAPTER 18

"Have you called them yet to set the date for your "caucus'?" asked Brad to Diric Omar.

"I have," answered Omar. "Croes Xuseen from the Seattle-Tacoma, Washington, Weaver Tafia from Amarillo, Texas and Arends Suleymann from Columbus, Ohio have all agreed to be here in Minneapolis at my Mosque on December 1 at 2:00 PM. I am still waiting for Oduber Geesi of Denver, Colorado to confirm."

"Get them on the phone and make any excuses you need. Also, Hussain Aaden from St. Cloud. Get all of them here in Minneapolis on that day. Our deal depends on it," Brad demanded.

"I understand Brad," answered Omar. "I will get them here. They understand that they must personally attend. No alternates and no excuses. They will be here. They are all captivated on how my people have been so successful and profitable in making money with our gambling, drug trafficking, fire arms trafficking, payments for security of local businesses, counterfeit goods and bulk cash smuggling. They want to observe and learn. They are just like me, greedy."

"Be careful what you say Diric. You don't want to end up with them. Let us run this show. Your role is to just follow our instructions. Then you'll be able to benefit yourself as well as help your community's assimilation into this County's culture and opportunities. This Country will never take away your community's traditions or religion. It's a win win for all of us. Remember, you were targeted by us specifically due to your ability to communicate and persuade. As long as you use those qualities during and after this operation is completed you will do very well for yourself and your community."

Diric Omar understood what Brad Carr was telling him. He didn't like it, but he knew the consequences of not cooperating with the FBI. He just felt that the deal he made with Brad Carr, was damaging his own people, in order to only benefit himself. These people who migrated to the United States for a better world should be allowed more than the United States was giving them. But he knew that was never going to happen. What he and his counterparts in other communities, around the Country, were doing was to aid and enrich the Somali community's wealth, culture and laws. But in effect, Omar turned out to be the naïve one. So he agreed to the arrangement he made with the FBI.

"By the way, Brad," asked Omar, "did you ever get your money that Kelly Walker took?"

"Not yet. But I will get it soon. No later than the first week in December after your 'caucus'. That's a promise.

Once Franken and Geil reached the downtown station, they immediately went to Chief Peterson's office. They had not asked one question about Fingal's gambling issue.

"Why in the Hell are you here in my office instead of canvasing all of the casinos as I ordered you to do?"

"Chief," Franken started, "Let us explain. Esmar and I have been discussing Fingal's suicide. You were at the mortuary when Alle Theil indicated that she had asked Dr. Woodcock to come to Aruba to perform a second autopsy on Ruiz. Alle Theil was Johm Ruiz's girlfriend. She was originally from a small town in Minnesota. Then she lived in Minneapolis for a while. Dr. Woodcock works at a Minneapolis hospital and works for the FBI as a consultant. Coincidence? I don't think so. Correct?"

"Maybe, but where are you going with this guys?"

Geil then said, "Chief, you spoke with FBI Special Agent for the Minneapolis office who indicated that he had sent Dr. Woodcock to Aruba. It wasn't Theil."

"Okay."

"So what if Alle Theil is either working for the FBI or is a confidential CI for them? Or maybe she just wanted some of the laundered money. Ruiz may have said something to her about the Walkers. More than likely she works for the FBI in some capacity. Otherwise why would she tell you she asked Woodcock to come to Aruba?"

Franken then added, "And wasn't it the FBI who told you that there may be some money laundering going through Aruba?"

"Go on," answered a skeptical Chief Peterson.

"Who would have benefited from Johm Ruiz's death? He was the most recent custom agent who always handled Bob and Kelly Walker when they went through customs. They may have been either bringing money here to the Island, or taking it out, or both. Maybe Alle Theil got close to Ruiz, either as a confidential CI, to get evidence of the money laundering, or maybe even attempted to get in on a cut of the laundered money. Maybe Ruiz was demanding a cut from the Walkers of the laundered money. After all, he was paying for his daughter to attend an expensive University in the States. He couldn't afford that on his salary."

"Go on," said the Chief."

"So either Alle Theil is an FBI informant, or Kelly Walker could have murdered Ruiz to stop his blackmailing of them for attempting to get a cut of the laundered money," said Franken. "If so, one of them wouldn't want Fingal to find out that Ruiz was murdered. One or both of them could have blackmailed Fingal to make sure his cause of death would turn out to be natural causes. Didn't you find out that Fingal never sent Ruiz's blood or tissue samples to the Curacao lab? Once Fingal found out about Dr. Woodcock wanting to do a second autopsy, Fingal panicked. Either he destroyed his fake reports and destroyed the blood and tissue samples, or Kelly Walker took them and ran away with them to the States with some of the laundered money."

Detective Geil then added, "Fingal knew he had screwed up the entire investigation into Ruiz's death. He would be caught once the authorities found out his reports and samples couldn't be found. His reputation was the most important consideration for him as a doctor and a person living on this Island. He had no choice but to commit suicide. Then no one would ever find out what he did."

"It's a little bizarre gentleman," replied the Chief.

"But is it worth investigating?" asked Franken.

"Detectives, you present several possible alternatives for both deaths, but I still have a gut feeling that Fingal's gambling had something to do with his suicide. Ruiz's death is different. Why would the FBI want a second autopsy? And I was the one who made the decision to have him cremated to help out his mourning daughter. Bad choice," said a frustrated Chief of Police.

"So where do you want us to go from here Chief?" asked Franken.

"Keep investigating your theories and also investigate the gambling issue. I'll make a call to Special Agent Taylor in Minneapolis and see if he knows where Kelly may be and what was in the black leather bag. And if he knows something more about this matter, maybe we can narrow our investigation."

Both detectives thought that the Chief would be more receptive to their conclusions. But now they had to actually start over. They had a lot of investigating to do. So they decided that first thing the next morning they would go back and interview Harrison Ramsey concerning the gambling issue. They also needed to interview Alle Theil concerning their other theories of the case. Even Fingal's wife needed to be questioned again. Maybe there was a marriage issue that could have caused the suicide. How did this investigation become so complicated?

Kelly was in her holding cell all by herself and was kept separated from all other inmates who were waiting for their arraignments. Kelly had no arraignment scheduled. What was the FBI's role in what she had been doing for the last several years? Why was the money she had hidden the government's money? She wanted answers but no one would speak to her. Kelly kept asking the guard for her phone call. Everyone incarcerated had the right to one phone call. But, Special Agent Taylor had instructed the guards to treat her well, but not to let her have any phone calls. He told them that she was an important CI and could not communicate with the outside world. She was to be treated well. She got the same food the guards ate or they brought her take out from close by restaurants. She had extra time to exercise outside, as long as it was by herself. But she could only speak with either Taylor or his partner Darius Clark. She continued to deny the whereabouts of the government's money until she was briefed on what she was involved in. She was stubborn.

Bob Walker continued to call Brad Nickolas and Marc Harper. Neither would answer their phones. Bob was frustrated and scared for his wife. Where was she? What was happening to her? He even called her supervisor at Super Value to see if she may have gone back to work. It was a long shot. But, he was told that she had taken a months leave of absence when she and Bob went to Aruba. Bob knew that, but he was desperate.

Bob, who was stressed out, felt he had only two options. Go to Marc's home and confront him. Or, go to 'Little Mogadishu' and confront Omar at the Mosque or cultural center. Bob knew that if he showed up at Marc's home, his family would be compromised since they had no idea what was happening. It would only cause a marriage dispute that may be disastrous. That he wouldn't do. So Bob drove to 'Little Mogadishu'. What he would say or do he had no idea. But someone had to give him some answers about the whereabouts of his wife. All of this was becoming unbearable to Bob.

Then Bob thought about his friend Harrison. What does he know about Kelly? What have the local authorities discovered? He must know something. He thought about calling him. If he knows something, that would allow him to stay away from Omar. Confronting Omar was Bob's worst scenario. So he called Harrison.

Harrison saw Bob Walker's name on his cell phone and answered the call. "Hello Bob. Are you back in St. Paul?"

"I am. But where is Kelly? Do you know? Marc Harper picked her up at the Minneapolis airport a couple of days ago."

"I have no idea where she may be. The local authorities are investigating both Ruiz's death and Fingal's suicide. I don' believe they have any idea about either one, or neither do I," lied Harrison.

"Dr. Fingal committed suicide?" asked Bob. "What in the fucking world is going on?"

"Cool it Bob. I don't know why Fingal is dead. Neither does anyone else. It seems that Kelly and Marc had a meeting with Brad Nickolas at some mall in St. Paul. He wanted the money that Kelly took when she left the Island. Brad claimed it was his money and not Omar's. Do you know what that was all about? Did she give it to him?"

"No, Marc told me he was instructed by both Brad and Kelly to leave the meeting. Kelly didn't have the money with her at the meeting so she couldn't have given it to him. Now no one seems to know where she is. I need to find her."

"Bob, the FBI is involved in this investigation in some fashion. I'm not really sure how or why. But what I do know is that Kelly wouldn't do anything without first thinking it through. She believes that there is much more to this scheme than we all know. She is probably holding the money as a hostage until she is told what is really happening and what the end game is going to be for all of us. You need to trust your wife. I'm sure she tried to contact you to let you know she is not in danger."

"She left me a note at our home, but that just stressed me out more. I need to find her. If you can't help, I will do this on my own."

Harrison attempted to talk Bob out of doing anything stupid. With the FBI involved, Harrison believed everyone would find out something soon. They are good at what they do. He wanted to let this work itself out. If Harrison or Alle Theil were arrested, Harrison promised to call Bob and Marc and let them know what the charges were. But Harrison didn't think that was going to happen. The last thing Bob needed to do was to confront Brad or Omar. Harrison wanted the FBI to take care of that. But Bob couldn't wait. Plus Bob questioned Harrison as to who Alle Theil was. Harrison told Bob to save that question for another time. She didn't affect him. Bob was mad enough that his own wife and best friend didn't trust him enough to inform him about what was happening for such a long time. Bob had become a determined man. His next stop was 'Little Mogadishu'.

CHAPTER 19

The next morning, Bob drove directly to the Cedar-Riverside area of Minneapolis adjacent to the University of Minnesota. He went directly to the Masjid Darul-Quba Mosque. He walked in and observed at least 50 men kneeling on a small prayer rug. They were reciting their daily prayers in Arabic. It was the Fajr prayer. That prayer starts off the day with the remembrance of God; it is performed normally before sunrise. Bob noticed Diric Omar performing his Morning Prayer along with fellow Somali members of the Mosque from the neighborhood.

Bob did not want to disturb them during their prayers. He left the Mosque and walked around the building and went into the cultural center. There he saw Brad Nickolas. He hadn't seen Brad since the episode on the beach in Aruba. At that time he was only known to him as John Smith. Bob walked up to Brad to introduce himself.

"I know who you are Bob," said Brad. But you don't know who I am."

"What do you mean? You're Brad Nickolas, Omar's right hand man in this scheme he forced us into. You have my wife and I want you to return her to me immediately."

"And you know this how?"

"Here is the note she wrote me which she left on my desk in my study before she met you and Marc Harper at some mall. She was to give you the money she took when she disappeared from Aruba."

Brad read the note. "Interesting. I wonder what Kelly knows. She certainly wouldn't tell me when I met her at the mall. But I don't care what she may or may not know about me or Omar. She wouldn't give me my money. I warned her that there would be consequences if she didn't comply. My instructions were specific, and the money belongs to the government of the United States and they don't like it if someone steals it."

"What are you talking about? How is our government involved? And who are you anyway?" asked Bob very confused.

"Do you know where the money is?"

"Of course not. I didn't even know how much money was involved until Marc Harper told me yesterday."

"Does Marc Harper know where the money is?"

"I doubt it. He was as confused and concerned as I am right now."

"Well, let's see how concerned your wife is?"

Brad took his cell phone out of his back pocket and dialed the Minneapolis downtown Federal Building. He asked the receptionist to connect him with the holding cell area. After a minute or so. Brad started speaking with one of the guards. They both asked each other about their families and discussed some other pleasantries. Bob had no idea what was happening. Finally Brad ask the guard to give his phone to Kelly Walker, the woman in the private cell. Now Bob was really stressed.

"Hello Kelly. This is Brad Carr."

Bob was stunned. Brad was just listening to some ranting by Kelly. Bob could hear her voice faintly coming from the phone but couldn't understand what she was yelling about.

Then Brad said, "I have your husband here with me. He also says he doesn't know where my money is. There will be more consequences for him unless you tell me where to find my money."

Brad slightly removed the phone from his ear as Kelly was yelling some obscenities and ranting again. Brad then said to Kelly, "I'll see you in about 20 minutes." Then he hung up.

"Well, since neither of you will tell me where my money is, I guess it's time for you to be brought into this operation. Turn around Brad and put your hands behind your back."

Brad was stunned. And afraid. With nothing else he could do he instinctively turned and put his hands behind him. Brad then handcuffed Bob and told him that he was going for a ride with him. Bob asked Brad again who he was. Brad told him that his real name was Brad Carr and he was an undercover Special Agent for the FBI. Bob was stunned.

"Am I under arrest?" asked Bob.

"No and I am not reading you your rights."

"I have rights. I want a lawyer."

"You're not under arrest and not being charged with any crime. So you don't need a lawyer."

Bob was now really confused and scared. Brad put Bob in the back seat of his car and drove him to the downtown Federal Building and parked in the underground lot. Brad then brought Bob to the holding cell area. Bob was uncuffed and required to remove everything from his pockets and give over his cell phone. He was told to take off his clothes and put on an orange jumpsuit. He was then taken to the cell where Kelly had been for several days. She was also in an orange jumpsuit. Bob couldn't believe what he was seeing. He was then put in the same cell as his wife. The door was locked and the last thing Brad said was that when they were willing to tell him where his money was he would then have them released.

"Kelly what in the Hell is happening to us?"

"Something big is going to happen and we are just in their way. I have been insisting we be informed of what exactly it is that is going on and how we fit into the government's plans. Brad Carr will not tell me anything, that's why I have not turned over their money."

"So you do know where their money is located. Does Marc know?"

"He may have figured it out, but I don't know. When Marc and I met Brad at the Rosedale mall, I put the black bag with the money in a locker at the mall. I gave the key to Marc and told him not to give it to anyone without my say so. He agreed."

"I still don't understand. Why not just give them the money instead of being a prisoner in this Hell hole?"

"We're not prisoners. We are Federal confidential informants. There has been some kind of sting operation going on over the last few years and we were recruited by Diric Omar to assist him and the government on this sting. I have no idea what it's about and why we were not told. They lured us based on our greed with their money we had been receiving monthly as well as the free trips to Aruba. Harrison and Marc were also recruited without their consent. That's all I can figure out so far."

"So this Brad Carr is a Fed? And he is working with Omar?"

"I believe he has made a deal with Omar for some kind of immunity or something else for all of the money he has collected over the last few years dealing with his unlawful fund raising actions. In fact, I believe, Omar hasn't really done anything criminal. The government has been helping Omar look like it was criminal. The government is probably funding everything including our cut."

"I don't believe it. There has to be more to it than that."

"Bob, Brad told me that I was one of his confidential CI's. I have been getting outside food and eating in the guard' mess for every meal. I am in a separate cell away from the real criminals. I get to go outside when I want. I use the woman guard's rest room. I just don't have a phone."

"So why don't you just give them their money?"

"They're going to need us for something soon. Until I know what's happening and the money we have been receiving doesn't have to be returned or declared income, I can wait them out in this three star hotel cell. I know they think I'll give in, but I want them to make me the offer. Not the other way around."

"You are crazy. I feel like I am in a 'who done it' movie."

"Just be cool. Things must be happening soon or Brad wouldn't have told me I was one of his CI's."

Bob sat down on the second bunk in the cell and laid down and put his hands over his face. What had Kelly got him into?

Alle Theil had just come home from work at the woman's clinic when she received a phone call. The area code was from the States. There was no name on her phone.

"Hello."

"Alle, this is Natasha. I just spoke with Kaydra. She received the proceeds of Johm's insurance policy. Thanks. So I see that you must have spoken with the lawyer I told you to see."

"I have. He has Johm's home and personal property up for sale. He obtained an Order from the Court making me the personal representative for the estate, just as you wanted. When all of those items are sold the proceeds will go to Kaydra."

"I told you everything would work out. Have you spoken with Kaydra?"

"Yes and we're getting along well. She'll be coming to Aruba for winter break. She'll stay with me. She doesn't suspect anything."

"Great. I'm glad for you. Kaydra is a great kid. She likes you a lot. Maybe someday she'll warm up to me a little more. Did you get the money I sent you?"

"I did. It was more than I thought you would send me. Thank you."

"There is more where that came from. I appreciate the fact that you and I could come to a beneficial agreement concerning that good for nothing abuser."

"I just seem to make bad judgments about men," confessed Alle.

"Well I'm glad Johm can't hurt you anymore. The longer you're with him the harder he hits and the more emotional pain he inflicts. He was always a charmer before he tied the knot. Just keep Kaydra believing he was a good father. The less she knows the better. Did you clean out Johm's refrigerator before the detectives and NCB got there?"

"I followed your instructions. I emptied the milk carton and took it home and burned it. I buried the cereal bowl and the spoon. No one will know that there was fentanyl in the milk. Johm loved his cereal. But the one thing I don't understand is why Dr. Fingal committed suicide? How did you arrange that?"

"Alle, I have no idea. On my mother's grave, I had nothing to do with that. I was as surprised as you. But, thanks for your help. Have a good time with Kaydra. We'll keep in touch."

Natasha hung up. Alle didn't believe Natasha about Fingal's suicide. But she didn't care. She was ready to start a new life.

Detectives Franken and Geil arrived at the Marriott Hotel the next morning to interview Harrison Ramsey again. This time they came with a Court Ordered Warrant for the casino's financials. They had warrants for 12 more hotel casino records located in the high rise area.

They went to the check in counter and asked the clerk to see Harrison Ramsey. They showed the clerk their badges and credentials.

"Has something happened?" asked the clerk.

"No, it's just a routine call. We need to speak to Mr. Ramsey about some people who have stayed at the hotel."

"Well I am sorry to tell you that Mr. Ramsey is not here right now."

"Can you tell us when he'll be back?"

"No, but if you would like to speak to his assistant, he is here."

"And who may that be?"

"He is Wells McSeffrey, the assistant manager."

"That would be great."

The clerk called the assistant manager and told him that two detectives were there to see Mr. Ramsey. Since Harrison wasn't there she told him that they would like to speak with him, if he was available. He told the clerk to bring the detectives to his office.

"Hello, I'm Wells McSeffrey, the assistant manager. May I ask what this is about?"

"Where is Harrison Ramsey?" asked detective Geil.

"He is at the airport. He is flying to Orlando. It is my understanding that the company may be promoting him to a regional manager in the Orlando area. Lucky man. What can I do for you?"

"That seems unusual. We just spoke with him a day ago and he never mentioned anything about a promotion."

"Well, that's the way things work in this business. Silence is golden. Nothing is ever for certain. I'm sure there are other candidates. But Harrison would make a fine regional manager. He is originally from the States, you know. I'm sure he would like to be back there."

"So, maybe a managerial job would be open for you if Ramsey gets the job?"

"Maybe. You never know in this business. Again, what can I do for you?"

"We have a Court Ordered Warrant for all of your casino records for the last year. We are specifically looking for a list of your 'high rollers' and for individuals or corporations that have lines of credit at the casino."

"Oh my! Let me see the warrant." Wells read the warrant slowly and wasn't quite sure what to do with it. Nothing like that had ever happened to him before.

"I think I need to call our lawyer about this," insisted Wells.

"You can do that," said Franken. "But first we want the records. You have read the Court Order."

"I'm not really sure what to do."

"Just give us your records and you can call whomever you like," said Geil.

Wells reluctantly went to his computer and brought up the 'high roller' list and all people or companies with lines of credit at the casino for the last 12 months. He then pushed the print key. About 30 pages of records printed out.

"I really think I need to call the hotel's lawyer," again insisted Wells.

"Go ahead and do that. You can keep the warrant to show your lawyer," said Franken.

Wells finally handed the documents to the detectives. Franken and Geil thanked the assistant manager and took the documents and left the hotel. The next stop was the Ritz Carlton.

CHAPTER 20

Brad Carr drove back from the downtown Federal Building directly to 'Little Mogadishu', after he had put Bob Walker in a holding cell. He had to finalize the sting operation with Diric Omar. This is the sting that Carr had been working on with Omar for over two years. It was imperative that it had to go exactly according to the FBI's original plan. The perfect place for it to happen was in the Masjid Darul-Quba Mosque in Minneapolis. All of the heads for finance and fund raising, including all of their accomplices, for their respective Mosques located in all of the major cities that have large Somali immigrant populations would be in the same place at the same time. That would amount to 45 Somali criminals. All of whom had been stealing, torturing and murdering their own people just to profit themselves.

The FBI had this operation as one of their top 10 undertakings nationally. Brad spoke with Omar to confirm that every one of the targeted members of their respective Mosques would be in 'Little Mogadishu' on December 1 at 2:00 PM. Omar assured Brad that he had personally spoken to each of the heads of the targeted Mosque. All agreed to be in Minneapolis at the appointed time. Brad had instructed Omar to emphasize that this caucus of leaders from the targeted Mosques privately to discuss how each of their operations could better improve their procedures to maximize their profits with less bloodshed.

Omar would be wired for sound and vision. 60 FBI agents from the Minneapolis, Chicago, Seattle Denver and Columbus office would be listening and watching from various mobile and stationary sites nearby. As soon as each of the heads of the targeted Mosques had verbally admitted to their crimes, a full-fledged raid would be made on the Minneapolis Mosque.

Omar had agreed to cooperate with the FBI only if he was charged with one misdemeanor and no jail time, and only community service. Brad had made those arrangements. The FBI, through Brad Carr, had been staging most all of Omar's criminal actions and funded most of them with government money which were transferred by Brad to offshore numbered accounts only accessible by Brad. All of that money, except for the money given to the hidden CI's including, Harrison Ramsey, Marc Harper, Bob and Kelly Walker, Irving Wernet and Alle Theil, would be returned to the government. The amount returned would be nearly $200 million for the Minneapolis area only.

All of the heads of the targeted Mosques and their accomplices would be tried for the violation of numerous Federal criminal laws and spend the rest of their lives, each in a different Federal prison. They would be required to sell all of their property and forfeit all funds they may be holding in offshore accounts. The FBI estimates that to amount over a $800 million dollars. A true triumph for the Feds.

Omar would also be arrested during the raid so as to not let any of the others attending the caucus to have any knowledge of Omar's cooperation with the government. His safety was to be protected if he needed to testify in any future trial that may be required. It was the hope of the FBI that a plea bargain could be reached by most, if not all of the persons arrested.

Omar was well coached by Brad Carr and all of the heads of the FBI offices involved in the raid. Omar was reluctant but cooperative due to the minute charges concerning the deal in which he agreed. Brad assured all of the FBI agents involved in the sting that Omar would not renege on his promises. He was frightened of an American Federal prison and the way he would be treated by the American inmates. Everything was worked out, to the minute, for the raid to occur on December 1. That date was coming quickly.

Detectives Franken and Geil had acquired a list of all of the 'high rollers' and people and corporations who had acquired a line of credit in 12 high rise area hotel casinos. Nowhere in any of those documents did the name Jan Fingal appear. The detectives thought that Fingal may have used an alias at one of the casinos. They spent a full day checking on all the names and where unable to find any alias for Fingal. There were 15 other casinos on the Island, but they were small and many locals frequented them. They were sure that Dr. Fingal would never take a chance on being spotted in a 'high roller' area of those casinos by a friend or colleague.

So the next day the detectives went to Fingal's home to interview his wife again. By that time the doctor had been cremated and a celebration of life was arranged by his wife and two children in the hospitals main conference room. Most all doctors and nurses who spoke had wonderful stories, some funny and some about his unique skill, as a doctor, and to take on extremely challenging cases. It was a sad day at Aruba's main hospital.

Fingal's wife confirmed again that the doctor had an impulse for gambling, but she was convinced that it was not an obsession, nor did he ever get himself in any financial trouble due to his gambling. The detectives reviewed all of the Fingal's financials, investments, income and liabilities, which Mrs. Fingal gave to them voluntarily. They searched the home and Fingal's office for any hidden safe that cash could be kept. They found nothing. Franken and Geil were certain that the Chief had them on a wild goose chase with his gambling theory. They had to convey that to the Chief by convincing him that they investigated every possible avenue dealing with a gambling problem.

After their interview with Mrs. Fingal, the detectives went to report their findings to the Chief.

"When you say that you investigated every possible avenue of gambling," started the Chief, "did that include interviewing every casino manager at the high rise area casinos?"

"No sir," said Franken. "But that would take weeks. And both of us, and his wife, are sure he was not a compulsive gambler. If anyone would know, it would be the wife."

"Could she be lying?" asked the Chief.

"What would be her motive? She is devastated that he committed suicide. She is as perplexed as we are. And you know the Fingals Chief. Do you believe she would lie to us?"

"Okay gentleman. Good job on that investigation. Now go ahead and pursue your possible theory concerning the girlfriend, Alle Theil. But good luck with that," said the Chief skeptically.

Brad Carr still could not break Kelly Walker as to the whereabouts of the half million dollars. Her husband pleaded with Kelly, but to no avail.

"You like rotting in this holding cell?' said Brad. If you don't talk, you'll be here until Hell freezes over."

"You need to either tell me what's going on and what our end game is or I will cause you a lot of trouble," argued Kelly. "And we want a lawyer and the ability to call one of our choice."

"I told you both that you're not under arrest and have committed no crimes."

"How about stealing half million dollars. Is that a big enough crime for you Brad?" retorted Kelly.

"Don't try to intimidate me Kelly. The best and brightest criminals have tried that for years. All you did was deliver the money to me, as a confidential FBI CI, so I could deposit it in an offshore account."

"Okay Kelly," exclaimed Bob. "Enough is enough. You're not getting anywhere with Brad. I'm going to tell him where the money is. I want out of here."

"Don't be an asshole Bob. Don't you see what Brad is doing? He has no intention to let us go after this sting or whatever he and Omar are planning. He has never told us that we will be free after this is all over. For all you know we're here until Hell does freeze over."

"That's not true Kelly. All I want is my money and you are both free to go and you'll never see me again."

"I don't believe you Brad. You have given us no reason to believe that you won't make us a part of your sting."

"Enough is enough," said Bob. "Marc Harper has the key to the locker at the Rosedale mall where the money is located."

"You asshole!" as Kelly slapped Bob's face. "I thought you had the balls to see this through. I can't believe you're the man I married. Harrison was right. If we had told you everything, from the beginning, about this scheme you would have gone to the authorities. That would have been disastrous for a lot of people."

"Finally a sane person," replied Brad. "When I get the black bag with the money I will be here and let you both go free. Thanks Bob. At least there is one sane person in your family."

Kelly turned her back to her husband and sat quietly on her bunk. Brad left the holding cell and went to the front office of the building. There he called Marc Harper. Marc's cell phone went to voice mail since he was at school teaching at the time.

Brad got in his car and drove to Cretin-Derham Hall High School. He walked into the administrative office and told the person behind the desk that there was an emergency and he needed to speak with Marc Harper.

"Has his wife been in some kind of accident? Are his kids Okay?"

"No they are fine. But it is imperative that I see him now." Brad showed the clerk his badge and credentials.

The clerk told Brad that she would go to his classroom and get him immediately. When she got to the classroom the freshman algebra class was just being let out. She went up to Marc and told him that an FBI agent was in the office and there was some kind of emergency and he needed to see him now. Marc was confused but went with the clerk back to the school office. There he saw Brad Nickolas.

"What is this emergency that brought you to my place of work?" Marc questioned Brad.

"Kelly gave it up. She agreed to a deal and she told me that she gave you the locker key at the Rosedale mall where my money is located. She told me to get the key from you. Do you have it with you?"

"I do, but I don't believe you. She told me to give you the key only when she personally tells me to."

"Well, until I get the key she is still in her safe place where she was placed until I got my money. So if you give me the key, I will take you to her and she can tell you herself. Then I will let both of you go on your way. After that you will no longer see me and our work will be complete."

"Are you telling me that this scheme we have been involved in all these years is now over?"

"That's what I'm saying. All the money you all received is yours and our work is complete. That's all you need to know. But I need that key first."

"But I still have several classes and practice left today."

"Make some arrangement with the school. I will have you back here in less than two hours. What do you say?" lied Brad.

Marc was very surprised. This was a different Brad Nicolas than the one at the mall. He thought about it for a few minutes, but he and Brad have had mostly a good relationship since the beginning of the scheme. He thought that there was no reason to question what he was now proposing. So Marc took the locker key out of his wallet and gave it to Brad. He turned to the vice principal of the school and told her that there was a small emergency that he had to attend to and that he would be back in a couple of hours. He asked her to have one of the other math teachers cover for him for his next class. The vice principal had no problem with that and told him that he hoped everything was okay. Brad assured her it was.

"Can I have that key now?" asked Brad.

"Shouldn't I wait until Kelly tells me to give it to you?"

"Give me a break Marc. We have got along for years. Why would I lie to you now? I just want to make sure that you are giving me the right information and key. You'll see Kelly in just a little while."

So Marc turned over the key to Brad. Marc then got into Brad's car and they drove to the Rosedale mall. Brad parked at the North entrance and told Marc to wait in the car. Brad went to the locker area and located locker 45. He put the key in the slot and turned it and opened the door. There was the black leather bag. Marc opened it and it was full of cash, some clothes and some makeup. He then went back to his car, put the bag in the trunk and got back in the car.

"Thanks Marc. You're a good soldier. Now let's go see Kelly."

Brad drove to the downtown Federal Building and pulled into the underground parking lot. He parked his car in his designated parking space and told Marc to come with him to meet Kelly.

"I don't understand," said Marc. "This is the United States Federal Building. Why are we here?"

"You'll see in just a minute. Follow me."

Brad took Marc to the holding cell floor and went into the reception area for prisoners. Marc started to stress out. What is happening, Brad?"

Brad called over to one of the prison guards and told him to take Marc Harper and prepare him for the special holding cell.

"What the hell are you doing to me," exclaimed Marc, as he was grabbed by his arm and shoved in a room.

When Marc came out he was in an orange jumpsuit. All of his clothes and everything in his pockets, including his cell phone, were in a plastic bag with his name on it. The guard was told to take him to the same cell where Kelly and Bob were located. When he got to the cell, Marc saw both Kelly and Bob, in orange jumpsuits. The guard unlocked the door and put Marc in the same cell and locked the door behind him.

Kelly wasn't shocked to see Marc. "Did you give him the locker key?" asked Kelly.

"Yup. He already has the bag and the money," said an embarrassed Marc.

"Shit! He conned you too," said Kelly pointing her finger at him. "He is a Federal Special Agent for the FBI. His real name is Brad Carr."

"What the Hell has been going on for all these years and what are we doing in a Federal prison? "Your guess is as good as mine," said Kelly. "He was supposed to release us when he got his money. And we still don't know anything about the scheme or the end game. I sure hope we're not looking at our end game."

"I am so sorry guys. I had no reason not to believe him. He has always been upfront with me."

"Well, it looks like he has never really been up front with any of us at any time. Now we just have to wait," said Kelly as she started to cry. Something she rarely did.

Brad went back to his car in the underground lot. Before he got into his car he made a call.

"Hello Brad," said the person on the other end of the call. "Is it done?"

"All three of them are in a nice cozy holding cell. They'll be well taken care of until after the December 1 raid. Then I will call in to have them let go."

"Do they have any idea of what's going down?"

"Not at all. They are really confused."

"Great, Call me when it's done and we'll met at the location we agreed. Then our new lives can finally start. Oh, by the way, did you get the half million dollars?"

"I did. And it was relatively easy."

"See you soon, Brad."

"Take it easy Harrison. Don't drink too much. We'll have plenty of time for that in a few days."

CHAPTER 21

Detectives Franken and Geil walked into the Aruba Woman's clinic where Alle Theil worked. They asked her supervisor, after showing her their badges and credentials, if they could have a few minutes with Ms. Theil. The supervisor approved the meeting as long as it didn't last too long. The detectives agreed to only take no more than a half hour.

Alle and the detectives then went into a conference room at the clinic and sat down.

"Why are you disturbing me at my work place? It's embarrassing. I try to help women who have psychological issues and if they see me with the police they tend not to trust me," said Alle.

"We are very sorry to have to do this here, but we need to try to wrap up the investigation on the death of John Ruiz and the suicide of Jan Fingal as quickly as possible. That's why we are here right now," explained Detective Geil.

"I thought that both of those matters had been finalized?"

"We're here Ms. Theil only to follow up and document a few open issues so that we can finalize our final report. We thought that you may be able to fill in some of those missing gaps by just answering a few questions."

"Okay. Let's get on with it. What do you want to know?" asked Alle.

"You and Ruiz were a couple, is that fair to say?" asked Franken.

"Yes, we had been dating exclusively for some time."

"Were there any issues with your relationship?"

"Like what?"

"Was Ruiz ever physical with you or emotionally abusive?"

"No, why would you even say that?"

"Do you know Ruiz's ex-wife Natasha Ruiz?"

"I met her at the mortuary when Johm's daughter, Kayla was making arrangements for his funeral. What would Natasha have to do with me? She lives in the States."

"Had you ever spoken with her before that meeting?"

"Of course not," lied Alle. "Where are you going with this?"

"Are you aware that the divorce papers filed by Natasha Ruiz against Johm Ruiz alleged physical and emotional abuse by her ex-husband?"

"No. I met Johm several years after the divorce. We never spoke about the particulars of his divorce."

"Was Kaydra aware of those allegations by Natasha?"

"Now you're going too far. Wrap this up detectives. If you think that I had something to do with Johm's death, just ask me."

"Did you?" asked Geil. "Chief Peterson thought that you and Natasha got along very well at the mortuary."

"Why don't you ask your Chief about who the person was who attempted to try to stop Johm's cremation on that day. I asked for another doctor to come to Aruba to do a second autopsy. I didn't believe Dr. Fingal's final report of death by natural causes. Why would I do that if I had anything to do with murdering him?"

"Actually, Ms. Theil, it was the Minneapolis office of the FBI who sent Dr. Woodcock to Aruba for the second opinion. Do you have a connection with the FBI? How do you know Dr. Woodcock?"

"I lived in Minneapolis for a while. I got to know several men while I was there. One of those men called me and asked me to find out if Johm actually died of natural causes. I was skeptical and asked why I would do that for him."

"Who is this man who called you? Did he work for the FBI?"

"His name was Brad Nickolas and no, he didn't work with the FBI. He may have known someone who did work for the FBI. Maybe they asked him to call me. I didn't ask any questions. Brad was a friend. So I told him I would do that. After all, I had nothing to lose. I had nothing to do with his death," lied Alle.

"None of that makes any sense," said detective Geil.

"It makes perfect sense to me."

Where were you when Johm Ruiz fell on his floor and died?"

"I was at home. Kaydra called me to tell me about Johm," again lied Alle. "I am done with any more questions. Obviously I can't shed any more light on the topic."

"Okay. Let's move on. Then how well did you know Dr. Fingal?"

"I didn't know him.

"You were seen speaking with him at Ruiz's celebration of life."

"That was the first time I met him. He wanted to know why I asked for a second autopsy on Ruiz's body. I stopped the conversation at that point and never spoke with him again. Gentleman, this interview is over. I am going back to work. I have women to help. I am sorry I may have wasted your time, but if you think that I had anything to do with Johm's death or Fingal's suicide arrest me."

Alle got up and left the room. She was there for 15 minutes.

The detectives both thought the interview was strange. If she was being abused by Ruiz and actually was involved with his death, why would she ask for a second opinion on the autopsy? Or was she forced to by this Brad Nickolas. Who was he? Did she date him? What was his connection with the Minneapolis FBI office? And who or what does the City of Minneapolis have to do with these two deaths? So many questions but no one left to ask them to. However, a call directly to the Minneapolis FBI office may be appropriate.

When the detectives got in their car, detective Franken called Ted Taylor, the Special Agent for the Minneapolis FBI office. The Chief and he had spoken a couple of times. It took several calls to reach Agent Taylor, but once they did, they explained who they were and asked if he would be kind enough to answer just a few lingering questions they had on several incidents that happen in Aruba which may be connected to their Minneapolis case. Agent Taylor agreed.

The questions dealt with why the Minneapolis FBI sent their medical consultant, Dr. Burton Woodcock, to Aruba to perform an autopsy on a customs agent where it had already been determined, by Aruba's coroner, that he died by natural causes. Agent Taylor told the detectives that the

FBI didn't send Dr. Woodcock to Aruba. Woodcock does consulting for the FBI. But they didn't hire him as a consultant in Ruiz's death. Taylor also didn't know anything, other than what their Chief had told him, about what was happening in Aruba.

Agent Taylor did reveal that he was involved in a large sting operation concerning several Somali communities throughout the States. The only connection between that sting and Aruba was questionable. However, Taylor thought that there may have been some money laundering involved with their sting operation which may had been laundered through Aruba in some unknown fashion.

"Do you know a Brad Nickolas?" asked Franken.

"He works for our office, but that is his undercover name. His real name is Brad Carr. He is working undercover for the Minneapolis office. I am unaware that he has been in Aruba. But when someone is undercover, our office loses contact with that person sometimes for weeks, or months, at a time."

"Do you know an Alle Theil who was originally from Minnesota? She lived in Minneapolis for some time before moving to Aruba. She may have dated Brad Carr."

"No, I don't know her. Who is she?" asked Agent Taylor.

"She was Johm Ruiz's girlfriend. That is the woman who claimed that she asked Dr. Woodcock to come to Aruba to perform a second autopsy on her boyfriend. Could she be an FBI undercover CI for Brad Carr?"

"I know Dr. Woodcock and I know he recently took a trip to Aruba, but I know nothing about what you're asking. I also don't know of any undercover CI, by that name. If Brad Carr has registered her with our office I would know her name. Do you believe she is an undercover CI that Carr is not telling me about? Or, is there some connection to our Somali community sting and Alle Theil? If so, I need to know."

"We don't think so. But even if we did we can't prove it. How do we get in touch with this Brad Carr?"

"You don't. He is still undercover. Our sting hasn't concluded yet. I have no idea where he is. Sorry I couldn't help. Wish I were with you in Aruba. If you ever want to change places, call me first. It's 12 below zero in Minneapolis today," then Agent Taylor hung up.

Both detectives were confused. Alle Theil knew Brad Nickolas, but not Brad Carr the FBI agent. Was she or Ruiz involved in some type of money laundering? Was she an undercover CI that Brad Carr didn't want to tell his office? Ruiz was paying for his daughter's education at some fancy University in Florida. How did he afford that? Was Theil giving him the money? Unfortunately, Agent Taylor seemed to hang up too quickly before those questions could be answered. Was that on purpose?

The detectives were going around in circles? Their inexperience was showing. They had already examined Ruiz's financials. There was nothing there. Maybe he was using laundered money from Alle Theil? But how could they find that out? And how did all the autopsy reports and tissues from Fingal's autopsy get lost? Did Kelly take them to the States? But why? How was she involved with Dr. Fingal? They just didn't have any good concrete answers. Someone was either very good at what they do, or the two deaths were what they had always been designated as originally, natural causes and suicide.

The detectives were tired and confused. Too many bizarre events in these cases where the dots just could not be connected. Time to do their final report and move on to the more mundane easy crimes committed on 'The Happy Island'.

CHAPTER 22

Harrison Ramsey and Brad Carr met during their first year in the hospitality graduate school at the University of Minnesota. Since Harrison and Bob were in different graduate schools at the University, Bob never really knew Brad. He met him several times when he was with Harrison, but they didn't socialize. That is why Bob didn't recognize Brad on the beach that day of the episode with Kelly. It had been years since Bob had seen Brad.

Harrison and Brad were both very ambitious and greedy. Sometimes they would sit and talk for hours about one day making millions of dollars and working together on some big exciting business deal. Brad, very quickly, became very bored in hospitality school. Law enforcement and weapons were more of Brad's liking. So after the first semester, Brad transferred from the University of Minnesota to the FBI Training Academy in Quantico, Virginia. That was much more of Brad's liking. However, Brad and Harrison kept in touch and spoke almost every week. They would meet in different parts of the Country for spring and winter breaks when they could arrange it. They always seemed to keep their hopes and dreams alive for making millions someday on that big and exciting business deal.

The FBI Training Academy taught many facets of law enforcement. The curriculum included academics which contained most general programs one would study in any graduate school concerning their program of study. Next was the intelligence training. That focused on basic and advanced training for intelligence analysts. Lastly there was the National Academy. That focused on the art of law enforcement and undercover work. Brad seemed to be a natural in the art of undercover work. He excelled in that portion of the curriculum so well, that once he graduated from the Academy, the Minneapolis FBI office recruited Brad to be an undercover agent right out of the Academy. Very few graduates were recruited for that type of work right out of the academy. But he showed such promise. He started as an FBI undercover agent solving and arresting interstate drug dealers. Next he was assigned to work on overseas weapons sales and interstate and Caribbean money laundering. He excelled on every case he was involved. He got high marks from all of his supervisors in each of his undercover undertakings. He had dozens of international criminals arrested and convicted. He brought in hundreds of millions of dollars to the government treasury on those criminal ventures.

Brad graduated the same year Harrison got his Masters degree in Hospitality. Both were disappointed that Harrison's first job was not in Minneapolis. Harrison was also disappointed that his other best friend Bob's first employment was in another state. But Harrison kept in touch with both. During those first years of employment Harrison, Bob and Brad never got together because Brad was always undercover. Harrison would go months without hearing from Brad during those first few years.

The year Harrison was promoted to general manager of the Aruba Marriott Hotel & Casino, Brad was assigned to an undercover sting operation dealing with several Somali communities throughout the United States. Since Brad had shown his supervisors his propensity for successfully handling undercover cases, the Minneapolis FBI office promoted him to Special Agent and put him in charge of this undercover case. Brad had the full authority to make any type of reasonable arrangement with the head of Minneapolis' largest Somali Mosque in 'Little Mogadishu'. The person who organized the Masjid Darul-Quba Mosque and was in charge of finances and fund raising for the Mosque and who also ran its criminal enterprises was Diric Omar.

Brad did his homework and used all of the resources of the Minneapolis FBI office to uncover the crimes being committed by Diric Omar and his accomplices as well as other leaders of Somali communities across the Country. Brad discovered the large amounts of money that their criminal enterprises were generating. There were also numerous injuries and several deaths that occurred in 'Little Mogadishu' and in other Somali neighborhoods around the Country. The carnage was much worse in the Somali communities outside of Minneapolis. Brad was given the authority to go undercover and investigate those incidents so he could attribute those matters to Diric Omar and other leaders in Somali communities in other locations around the States.

Brad had been threaten by several coconspirators of Omar when he asked probing questions to people in Omar's community. It was difficult for Brad to obtain sufficient evidence to arrest Omar for the numerous crimes sanctioned by him against his own people. This included crimes against outsiders near the Somali community who would not comply with the Mosque's criminal fund raising methods. People, both Somali and US citizens, were terrified to speak to a Federal officer about what their own community's religious leaders were doing to them. However, with the promise of possibly being able to enter the witness protection program and an immediate Visa to whoever talked, Brad tactfully was able to obtain written affidavits, and promises to testify, against Omar and his associates. That included Somali business men, residents and other outside business people who were forced to pay money for security so their business wouldn't be robbed or damaged by Somali gangs who answered to Omar.

Also, people who were charged outrageous fees and interest for loans that could hardly ever be repaid gladly sought the help of the FBI with the promise of the witness protection program. The most people who were anxious to testify were those whose under aged children where used by their religious leaders as sex slaves and domestic slaves.

Once all of the evidence was compiled and verified it was provided to Brad's supervisors at the FBI. The plan that Brad had put together to make a deal for Omar to stop those practices, not only in Minneapolis, but to require Omar to help the FBI stop those practices in other Somali communities around the States was a go for the Minneapolis FBI office to head the investigation and ultimate arrest of those responsible.

Brad was given full authority to undertake his plan. He could utilize as much resources necessary from the government, including man power and money to make any arrangement necessary for those types of practices to stop. Brad had finally reached the highest goal as an undercover Special Agent for the FBI. His operation could amount to just under a billion dollar sting. It was now time to confront Diric Omar and either arrest him or persuade him to cooperate and to take down all of the corruption in the largest Somali communities across the Country.

On September 15, 2018, just two years before Johm Ruiz died, Brad Carr and a troupe of FBI agents, under Brad's direction, entered the Masjid Darul- Quba Mosque and confronted Diric Omar. This was accomplished in-between prayer sessions. Omar was all alone at the time. Brad walked up to Omar and asked him if he knew who he was. Omar said that he knew that he and others were questioning members of his Mosque and the Somali community.

"My Name is Brad Nickolas. I am in charge of the undercover FBI unit for the Minneapolis FBI office. You are Diric Omar. You are the head of this Mosque and this Somali community. You call yourself the finance director and fund raiser for the Mosque."

"That is correct. So what does the FBI undercover unit want with me?"

"Mr. Omar, I am here to arrest you and your co-conspirators for numerous crimes committed by you and your associates against the residents of your community and other resident of the City of Minneapolis. I have an overabundance of evidence connecting you with crimes dealing with gambling, assaults and battery, illegal payments for bogus security of businesses, loan sharking and using under age children for sex slavery and other associated crimes. You and your associates will spend the rest of your lives in a Federal penitentiary. Do you want to see the warrant for your arrest?"

"No. That will never happen. I am the Somali high priest for the people in this community. No one in this community will believe anything you say. I am trusted with continuing to teach my people to live their lives through our culture and laws. No one in this community will help you take me away."

Brad then opens a small leather case and takes out dozens of written statements, affidavits, pictures and bank statements. He sets them in front of Omar. He looked at the plethora of evidence that convinced Omar that the FBI had done its due diligence before this confrontation. As a smart man, Omar looked at Brad and said, "Can we speak alone?"

Brad told his agents to stand down. He and Omar went into the adjacent cultural center and sat at one of the oblong tables with cash counting machines on it.

"What a unique room for a non-criminal," said Brad.

Omar ignored that comment and looked directly into Brad's eyes and said, "You said you were in charge of an undercover unit for the FBI, correct?"

"That is what I said."

"Is there a deal to be made here? How can I help you so that you can help me?" said a stressed Omar.

"Who said anything about a deal? What is it that you may have that could benefit the United States government? You saw my evidence. What else is there to say? You are coming with me downtown to a Federal holding cell. You, and your associates in the Mosque, are under arrest."

"I do have something your government may be very interested in," said an Omar that believed he could get out of any predicament.

"This I have to hear," said a confident FBI agent who knew what Omar was going to say. Brad was doing exactly as he was taught in school and in real undercover situations.

"There are at least 5 other Somali communities in several states, including here in St Cloud, Minnesota, who are committing more atrocious crimes than any committed by me in this community. I respect the majority of this community. There are only a few bad apples, as you Americans say. Those are the ones I pray on. As to the other communities, I can get each of their religious community leaders to admit their crimes which are much worse than this community. Also, they will reveal the locations where they hide the money that they use to enrich themselves on the backs of the Somali people in their communities. But first, I need some assurances from you and the FBI that I will get full immunity for any of these crimes you are alleging that I have committed."

"Omar, I don't trust you. How do I know you can do what you say you can do? And where is all of the money that you and your associates have hidden to enrich yourselves for your actions you have perpetrated on your community and the people of Minneapolis? And even if you can convince me, full immunity is out of the questions. Too many Somali people in this community have been hurt, lost their business or their accumulated wealth. Full immunity is out of the question," said a savvy agent who was reeling in a future undercover confidential informant. "Tell me exactly what you can do for me."

Omar thought about it. He sat down and started to think about his friends that he would have to give up. A Somali high priest giving up other Somali religious comrades. But then an American Federal prison was not something Omar could live with. He then looked at Brad and asked, "If not immunity what are we talking about. I can't do prison time," said a humiliated Somali man.

"If you can do what you say, and you let me be your right hand man, I can set up fake crimes in this community and you will publicize them as real crimes. The government will fund the money for those crimes and the government will keep the money that are proceeds of those crimes. I will completely control where the money goes. You will receive only enough money to keep the Mosque running and a small stipend for you to live your life as if no undercover action is going on." Brad continued, "All your associates will surrender themselves to the Federal authorities to be charged with lessor crimes. But will agree to a plea agreement with the local Federal Attorney General and do at least three years in the local Federal prison, or until the final raid has been completed and all of the other Somali leaders committing crimes are arrested, convicted or agree to plea deals and locked up in a Federal prison. That may take some time. No one from the neighborhood, including your associates will know that I am an FBI agent. I am just being hired by you to advance your control and further enrich you. You must have your counterparts, in the other communities, meet at least twice a year in some location, to discuss the crimes in their communities and reveal where their money is located. All of that must be obtained by you being wired for voice and video. The last meeting, in a couple of years or earlier, if possible, will be at your Mosque here in Minneapolis. The FBI will raid this Mosque and arrest everyone at your caucus. You will also be arrested and put in a holding cell until you testify against these other community leaders. You will be charged only with several lesser misdemeanors. No jail time. Only community service. That community service can be done in your Mosque supervised by me. Can you do that?"

"That is one big ask."

"You have one minute to agree, or you and your associates will be coming with me today and charged with all possible charges so you spend the rest of your life in Federal Prison."

Omar thought for a few seconds and finally said, "I agree. I don't like this. I hope we can work together. You are going to need people to assist you to launder the money that the government will fund for these false crimes. All the other community leaders will have to know that I am still making money on these transgressions. After all, some of the money is used to enhance the community and give scholarships to deserving children of Somali decent."

"You must know some outsiders who will do you a favor that we can recruit without them asking questions and still believe that these transgressions are really happening."

Omar thought for a few minutes. Then he remembered a few years ago when a group known as 'SALT' came to try to assimilate his community into the culture and laws of Minneapolis. Brad listened to Omar's story about these college students from the University of Minnesota and St. Thomas University who would probably now have jobs all over the country. They had promised to do Omar a favor if he required them to do it. There was also a woman who I scared out of one of my buildings. She was counselling my young Somali woman. Brad couldn't believe that any of those people would just do a favor for Omar so many years later.

"Do you remember their names?" asked Brad thinking that it would never work.

"I believe the people who were in charge of the 'SALT' group and made that promise to me were Harrison Ramsey, Marc Harper and some girl named Kelly. The other woman was Alle Theil. She is in Aruba now. I have been following them for years."

Brad could not believe what he just heard. Could this be the same Harrison Ramsey he knew? He went to the University of Minnesota as an undergraduate. How many Harrison Ramsey's could there be? His best friend, Bob Walker, married a girl named Kelly. What a coincident. If that were true, Brad remembered his and Harrison's dream about the two of them making millions of dollars someday by finding some unique business deal. But Brad was in law enforcement. How could he profit from this sting? He needed to talk to Harrison.

"Omar, which one of those four people would be the person you can scare the most to get them to handle laundering the money?"

"No question. Marc Harper. But Alle Theil now lives in Aruba and she has been the girlfriend of a custom agent on the Island. That may help. I follow all of the people who have agreed to do favors for me."

"Let's see if any of these four people will actually do you a favor. I'll have our agreement legally drawn up on paper. I'll need my supervisor to sign off. I will also need a dozen or so Somali FBI agents to assist you and me for this sting. That should be easy. Meantime, I will take all your associates being held in the Mosque, downtown to Federal holding cells for an arraignment. Let me know what this Marc Harper says. Maybe we may be going into business together. You better be telling me the truth. The FBI will be keeping tabs on you. The rest of your life depends on this."

CHAPTER 23

Brad Carr contacted his supervisor immediately after he and Omar made their deal concerning the sting. He explained the entire operation to his supervisor and estimated that the sting would clean up 95% of all Somali crimes throughout the country. Brad told his supervisor that he would start to go undercover immediately as Omar's main assistant and handle all of the fake crimes in 'Little Mogadishu'. Brad asked for as many FBI agents of Somali origin the supervisor could find to assist him with the sting operation. That was no problem. Most important for Brad was an assurance that he would be the one who would handle all of the sting proceeds. He would arrange for all of the deposits and withdrawals of the money. This included any funds that the government would authorize use of for any of the crimes.

Brad also insisted that there had to be some real crimes committed by Omar, or the undercover FBI agents, but only non-violent ones. Omar and the undercover FBI agents would steal money by shaking down businesses in return for security from robberies or trashing their businesses. The gambling, including table games such as blackjack and craps as well as sports betting would continue. The granting of high interest rate loans would also stay active. Without those activities, it would be too obvious that something unusual was happening in Omar's territory.

Brad insisted that he would be the only person to handle and launder the money on those crimes also. Omar would only receive enough money from the proceeds of those crimes to fund the operation of the Mosque.

And the final assurance was that no one would be seriously hurt or killed during any of the fake or real crimes.

"Sounds good to me," said Brad's supervisor, David Scrivens. "Text me all the terms of your deal and I will get the lawyers to memorialize it on paper. I will also requisite the dozen, or so willing Somali born FBI agents so you can start the sting. By the way, what is your undercover name going to be this time? Or, do I need to ask?"

"Same as always, Brad Nickolas," laughingly said Brad. "I'm also going to need several undercover CI's to make the laundering of the money look more realistic. Omar has indicated to me that some naïve liberal kids, who now live in several states with one even living in Aruba, had previously promised him a favor. A few years ago, when these kids were in college, they asked Omar to allow them to meet with as many consenting people in his Somali community to clarify and educate them as to the requirements to becoming assimilated into the culture and laws of Minneapolis. Omar agreed to their requests on certain conditions. One of those conditions was that they promised to do him a favor, with no questions asked, when requested. You can imagine how that went over. Omar scared them to death. They will be perfect for this sting. I'll pay them just enough CI money to keep them interested. They won't even know they're our CI's, or that this case is even a sting."

"Sounds complicated but also too good to be true. If we're able to take down all of the corrupt leaders in all of these Somali communities around the Country, it will be a huge win for the FBI including for you and me. I'll get things started on my end. Good luck and stay safe. Probably won't be speaking with you much during the sting. You know how to solicit your seed money. Use it wisely."

"Thanks boss. You can trust me. We'll get them all. It may take some time and money, but it will save many lives and hopefully be the catalyst to bring the American Somali population into our culture and laws in a legal and humanitarian manner."

After Omar and the FBI signed the legal document outlining the sting and arrangements for the ultimate charges and sentencing for Omar, all of Omar's associates were arraigned in Federal Court. They were remanded and all agreed to a plea deal. All was done secretly so it wasn't obvious to the people in the community. The plea deal indicated that the associates would only be imprisoned in a minimum secure Federal prison until after the sting was successful. All of the associates agreed to those terms. Only a maximum of approximately three years was a good deal in their minds. Especially after what Omar had demanded of them. This was Omar's co-conspirator's agreement with the FBI for them instead of 25 years to life. Once the sting was successful, they would be let go with no parole and time served. Good deal all around.

Undercover FBI agents, who were of Somali decent, were then assigned to Brad to assist Omar on the sting. Omar's legal agreement, and the co-conspirator's agreement would be binding only if the sting was a success. Omar was not happy, but a willing participant to save himself from doing any Federal prison time.

Thereafter, when the FBI undercover agents moved in to work for Omar, he made it clear to his community that his fundraising for the Mosque and cultural center, as well as for community projects would not change. He was just making some personnel changes to handle the fund raising and make the operation more efficient. This was announced at the Mosque and spread through the community quickly. No one quite understood what that meant, but it didn't change their fear and anxiety towards Omar.

When the sting finally became legally binding, three things happened.

First, Omar made a call to Marc Harper. That call terrified Marc. It took him several minutes to even remember Omar's rules allowing 'SALT' to continue counseling Somali community members. All Omar requested Marc to do was to get his other two 'SALT' committee members to help him move some money around several banks in the Caribbean and to do some errands for his associate, and right hand man, Brad Nickolas. Brad would be in charge of Marc and his friends. Omar indicated that they all were going to be paid well for their cooperation. Marc was told that his contact person, for moving the money or other errands, would only be Brad Nickolas. However, if anyone, who was not the three students on his committee, happened to come in contact with Brad, they must be told by that committee member that Brad's name was John Smith. No one but the 3 committee members were to know Brad's real name. Marc didn't understand that but didn't ask any questions. Marc was terrified and knew what would happen if he didn't follow Omar's request. So reluctantly he agreed to try to convince Harrison and Kelly to go along, imagining the consequences if he didn't.

Second, Omar called Alle Theil. She was told it was time for her to do Omar that favor she promised him when he gave her the seed money she used to move to Aruba. She needed to form a relationship with a custom agent or two in Aruba so certain people, whose names she would find out soon, would be able to pass through customs without ever being searched. She would be paid well for her favor. So long as she did what she was told, everyone connected with her life would be safe. Alle never believed that Omar would ever find her after she left Minneapolis. She was terrified and asked how she was supposed to accomplish his request. He told her that she was a very resourceful person and if she wanted her family in Northern Minnesota to remain well, she would agree to do this favor. He reminded her about the money he gave her in Minneapolis and told her that she would be compensated well again for agreeing to do this favor. He again repeated his threat. How did he find her? But he did and he continued to terrify her, just as he did in Minneapolis. She finally also reluctantly agreed.

Third, Brad Carr called Harrison Ramsey.

'Hello old friend," said Brad. "Congratulations on your promotion to general manager of the Aruba Marriott Hotel & Casino. We haven't spoken for some time. I've been undercover for years on various FBI matters."

"I am really glad to hear your voice. I thought about you many times. I'm sure your undercover work has been very dangerous. Glad to hear your fine. Are you finally through with that undercover business?"

"Not really," remarked Brad. "I have just been promoted to Special Agent for undercover work at the Minneapolis FBI office. I have also been placed in charge of a huge undercover sting operation. One that involves hundreds of millions of dollars. Remember our many discussions, years ago, about someday finding a large business deal where we could do little work and make millions of dollars?"

"Of course. I'm still wishing that may happen someday."

"Well my good friend, maybe it has."

"What do you mean?"

"Let me tell you a story. You may just think that it is a huge coincidence, but trust me, it's not."

Brad then told Harrison about Minneapolis' 'Little Mogadishu' that was going to be the location of Brad's next undercover sting. He indicated that there were at least a half dozen other 'Little Mogadishu's' all around the United States that were committing much harsher crimes against their own Somali populations and US citizens and businesses that were located close by. The man who would be Brad's undercover contact and cooperate with Brad to apprehend all of those Somali criminals was Diric Omar. Harrison thought for a moment and then was stunned when he remembered that name.

Brad told Omar that he needed some outside people to help him launder the money that would be collected during the sting. The money laundering was going to start by depositing money in several Aruba banks. Right where Harrison worked. After that money had been inactive for a few months, it would be withdrawn and deposited in other banks all around the Caribbean. He then explained how the sting would apprehend all of the Somali criminals from the 'Little Mogadishu's' outside of Minneapolis. The Minneapolis criminals have already been imprisoned by Brad. The only one left to deal with was Diric Omar. For no jail time, Omar had consented to be part of the sting. Hundreds of millions of dollars were being extorted by the other Somali criminals.

Harrison interrupted Brad and said, "I know Diric Omar."

"I know that. That's why I'm calling you before you get a call from Marc Harper."

"Wow! Another name from my past."

Then Brad went on to explain how Omar remembered that Harrison, Marc Harper and some woman named Kelly agreed to do Omar a favor someday. So Brad made arrangements for Harrison and his old friends to be in on the sting. That would be the favor they owed Omar. Harrison and his friends would be transporting the money Brad takes from the sting to Aruba and back to Brad so he can deposit the money in secure numbered accounts in offshore banks. Harrison listened carefully and then started to panic.

"You're telling me that I will be doing undercover work for the FBI?"

"That's what I'm saying. And the FBI wants to compensate you for doing this. It won't take much time from your current job. But that's not what I'm thinking. I want to ask you a confidential question. It's a question that I will deny I asked you to my dying day."

"You know me well, Brad. This conversation never happened."

Brad then went on and explained to Harrison that it would take a couple of years for the sting to fully play out. The plan on apprehending all of the criminals was already in play. Brad had complete control of all of the money for the sting. So instead of the money ending up in offshore Caribbean banks, Brad would be depositing the money in a dozen numbered accounts in different banks in Switzerland.

When the time comes that all of the Somali criminals were apprehended, Brad would be in a Country that does not extradite people back to the United States. Brad, and only Brad, would have control and knowledge of the whereabouts of hundreds of millions of dollars. Once the sting was fully explained, Brad asked Harrison to be part of Brad's own personal sting on his employer, the FBI. Their long time wishes would then come true.

Harrison was even more stunned. The first thing he thought of saying was, "Brad we would be international criminals on the run. They would know who we were. We could never get away with it."

"Harrison, during one of my undercover missions I met, and made very good friends with a man who makes perfect fake documents. He lives in a Country in Asia, which shall remain nameless. We would have all of the fake passports, driver's licenses, birth certificates, credit cards and social security numbers we need to change our identities, back and forth, at any time. The money will be in banks under multiple names. Believe me, I have thought this through. I can even have perfect fake bank account documents made up for the FBI to review as too where the governments money is located. It will work. In fact I am going to have some fake passports made up for one of your friends, Ms. Kelly, whatever her last name is, for her to use if things go bad during the sting. If she is in Aruba, and there is some confusion concerning the sting, she is the one that needs to come and see me. I can make that happen. I will be able to handle her. I have handled the worse criminals while I was undercover. She will be easy to manipulate. For whatever reason she needs to leave, she will be able to get off the Island under an assumed name. The FBI will never know. Also, if she has to leave for any reason, I don't want customs to know her real name. I understand that she was the brains of your young group. That's why I picked her. I hope you take no offense. Also you are working in Aruba and I wouldn't want you to leave Aruba until the Somali sting was over."

"No offense taken. But how do we get the money in and out of Aruba? There are customs in both directions, you know."

"Omar will take care of that. He has other people involved in the sting who owe him a favor. You don't need to know their names. You'll hear all about it from Marc."

"I need to think about this. You're talking about the rest of our lives. Maybe I'll never be able see my family or friends again."

"Nothing is perfect, Harrison. But what a life we could have. No work schedule. Just a large yacht, huge homes, women galore and every want and need taken care of. We can change identities, back and forth, dozens of time as we need to. Just think about it. You don't need to make a decision right now. We can finalize everything over the next few months. The sting will last a long time. So if you decide not to do this with me I'll understand. But I am all in. With or without you. I trust you completely to cover my ass. By the way, my name under the sting is Brad Nickolas. If we see each other in Aruba for any reason, act like we never met. You'll find out about all that, as well as your other duties, from Marc Harper. Act surprised when he calls you. Just remember, no matter your final decision, we never had this conversation."

Brad then hung up.

Harrison was in a complete fog. What just happened? Harrison never thought that the big business deal that would make him millions of dollars would be criminal. Could he go through with it? Brad is smart and Harrison loves adventures, but wow!

Over the next couple of years the sting went on with Omar and Brad working undercover. Nothing changed in Minneapolis' 'Little Mogadishu' and the crimes went on. There was gambling everywhere in the community. High interest rate loans were given out to anyone in the community that needed it. If the payments weren't made, threats were made and 'sort of carried out'. Businesses were forced to pay money for security to stop them from being robbed or trashed. Some people got hurt, but not badly. Some businesses were robbed if they refused to pay, but, again, no one got hurt seriously.

All of the money from those criminal activities where then given to Marc Harper from Brad. Marc then gave the money to Kelly Walker. Her and her husband, Bob, would then take free trips to Aruba and stay at The Aruba Marriott & Casino. Harrison Ramsey was their connection in Aruba. They were told to look for a certain custom agent when they arrived and left Aruba. That person's name was revealed to them before each trip.

All of the money was then transferred from Kelly to Harrison who put them in several Aruba Banks under false names, with credentials supplied by Brad Carr. Brad would also come to Aruba and stay at a hotel, away from the Marriott, so no one knew he was there, not even Harrison. He would take the money that had been dormant in Aruba banks, for a few months, and transfer that money to numbered Swiss Banks under one of his or Harrison's fake names. Brad's monthly reports to the FBI falsely indicated that the money was being transferred into offshore Caribbean accounts. Brad's connection, in Asia, would make false bank statements if they were required to be given to Brad's supervisor. The statements were so perfect, no one could tell that they were false.

While the sting was happening, Omar made arrangements to meet with all of the leaders of 6 Somali communities around the United States. They met at different places each time. Omar was wired for sound and video each time. The Somali leaders made a weekend of it and enjoyed themselves. But, there was always a business meeting where each of the leaders would discuss their criminal enterprises, how much money they had collected and where the money was located.

All of this went on for nearly two year until the day Johm Ruiz was found dead. That event stunned Brad, the FBI, and each of the undercover CI's except Alle Theil. That event was the catalyst for Kelly Walker to decide that something unusual was happening. Murder was not part of this scheme. Johm was one of the custom agents that Kelly and Bob used when going through customs. Too much of a coincidence. That is when Kelly decided to 'borrow' some of the sting's money, use the fake passports she found in her fanny pack, and leave Aruba to confront Brad Nickolas.

That was a mistake Kelly was to regret. It caused her, her husband and Marc Harper to end up in a Federal holding cell. Brad Carr was greedy. He used every tool he had to get the money Kelly took from her Aruba hotel room. He wasn't going to leave that money on the table somewhere. Once Brad finally attained the borrowed half million dollars and had the three CI's in a holding cell, it was time for Brad to finalize his own sting against the FBI.

CHAPTER 24

It was December 1, 2002. Diric Omar was hosting all of the heads of the largest Somali Communities and Mosques at the Masjid Durul-Quba Mosque. It was one of their periodic meetings. Omar was following the instructions of Brad's sting. Croes Xuseen from Seattle-Tacoma, Washington; Weaver Tafia of Amorello, Texas; Arends Suleymann of Columbus; Ohio, Oduber Geesi from Denver; Colorado and Hussain Aaden from St. Cloud, Minnesota were all present along with all of their criminal associates.

During the prior two days, they had all been enjoying the culture, entertainment centers and restaurants of the Minneapolis area. But on that day it was time for their usual business meeting. Each of the leaders of their Mosques gave a report on their current criminal activities, the amount of money pilfered and where they were depositing their ill gained funds. In that meeting, sitting next to Omar, was Brad Nickolas, Omar's first in command under the arranged sting.

Just 100 yards away from the Mosque were stationed 25 FBI agents and 50 City of Minneapolis swat police officers. One of those FBI agents was Brad Carr's supervisor, David Scrivens. He was in charge of the sting operation that night. He was in a van listening to the conversation and watching the video that was being recorded of the business meeting through the wire Diric Omar was wearing. After each of the Mosque leaders finished their presentation, it was time for the host, Diric Omar to give his report. That was the appointed time that all of the FBI agents and the police officers were to raid the culture center. A Federal Warrant had been obtained for the arrest of every Mosque leader and their criminal assistants including Diric Omar. Brad Carr had given his supervisor the names of every person attending the business meeting that evening.

Several days prior to the December 1 meeting, Harrison Ramsey flew from Orlando, Florida to Minneapolis. Harrison had told his assistant manager that he was going to Orlando for a week to attend a manager's conference. There was no such conference. He didn't return to Aruba. From the airport Harrison took the Marriott Hotel shuttle to the Downtown Marriott Hotel just blocks from where the new Minnesota Twins stadium was built. It was in the heart of downtown Minneapolis. The Hotel was 28 stories, had 675 rooms and 25 suites. The evening Harrison checked in and showed the check in clerk his credentials, as the Manager of the Aruba Marriott & Casino, he was provided a suite on the 28th floor. That evening Harrison checked in, he had a visitor. Brad Carr came to his suite.

As Brad walked in the room he said, "Nice digs my friend."

"Well, I do have some pull with the management of the hotel," commented Harrison.

"Are you ready for our lifetime adventure?" asked Brad.

"I'm here aren't I?"

"The raid will occur on the evening of December 1. I will be there. As soon as the culture center is raided, there will be chaos. I will sneak out one of the doors during that chaos and catch a cab to the airport international terminal. I have already made arrangement for the ride. I will meet you at the gate for an 8:45 flight to Geneva, Switzerland. Here is your boarding pass," as he handed it to Harrison. "From there I have booked two rooms at the La Reserve Genève-Hotel & Spa. Its 30 minutes from the airport and a 30 minute walk to downtown Geneva. We have an appointment on December 2 to see a banker about transferring some money from the Banco Santander International SA bank to several other banks. We'll withdraw $50,000.00 cash each as walking around money. Here is your passport with your new identity. That new identity was the name on Harrison's boarding pass. I have Federal Expressed all of our other documents to the manager of the hotel. That includes multiple passports and fake credit cards under each of our aliases. I have made arrangements for all documents to be delivered to a Post Office box at the bank in Geneva. We can pick up all of those documents when we arrive. Everything is set. I have thought through every contingency. It's been two years for me to figure this out. Nothing will stop us now."

Brad walked to the bar in Harrison's suite and took out two miniature bottles of Jack Daniels. He put some ice in a low ball crystal glass and poured both bottles into the glass. "This is your last chance to get out of this adventure. But you know there is no turning around for me."

"I'm here aren't I?" said Harrison again.

"Great, you and I will make good companions," as he drank the glass of Jack Daniels. "See you in a couple of days at the airport. Enjoy downtown. I'm sure you remember where all the good restaurants and bars are located. After all, you were born in this town"

Brad left the hotel. Harrison was still terrified.

After all of the leaders of the Mosques spoke, Omar started walking to the podium to give his report. Just as Omar started to speak, all 25 FBI agents and half of the Minneapolis swat police officers stormed the cultural center. Both doors leading into the cultural center from the outside and two doors to the Mosque were slammed open. 25 of the swat police officers were positioned outside the doors and windows in case any of the Somali leaders or criminal associates attempted to flee the premises.

David Scrivens watched the entire raid from an FBI van parked a block away. The van was a modified Ford van, equipped with two ergonomic seats for comfort, cameras inside and outside the van, video machines capturing the entire raid from several angles, voice controlled cell phone capability and microphones enabling Scrivens and his FBI agents and the Minneapolis police officers to communicate with the agents conducting the raid.

"Federal agents, everyone on your knees and put your hands up over your heads," yelled one of the agents as the culture center was being stormed. Chaos followed. Most of the perpetrators acquiesced to the agents command. However others ran to one of the doors or attempted to open a window. Several tried to hide under tables and behind curtains.

Everyone who attempted to escape was eventually apprehended and handcuffed. Not a shot was fired. When all 45 attendees at the meeting were finally handcuffed, they were put into a circle on the floor of the culture center. That included Diric Omar. All of the Somali Mosque leaders and their associates, other than the undercover Somali FBI agents, were then ushered, in a single line, into several prison vans that drove up to the Mosque just after the raid. All except one, Brad Nickolas.

Prior to the raid, each FBI agent and all of the Minneapolis swat police officers were given a picture of Brad Carr. He was not to be touched during the raid. As the prison vans were transporting the perpetrators downtown to the Federal holding cells, Brad got into his prearranged cab and drove to the Minneapolis/St. Paul International airport terminal. There he was to meet Harrison Ramsey. On his way to the airport, Brad called the Federal holding cell office.

"Hello, Minneapolis Federal prison," answered the officer in charge."

"Hey Tommy, This is Brad Carr, badge number 17896. The raid on the Minneapolis Mosque just went down. It went much smoother than I thought it would. Very few of the Somali perps resisted. None of them even had a weapon on them. Give my regards for a good job to David. You should be receiving about 45 or so prisoners in a few minutes."

"I just got the call from David," said Tommy. "He said the same. Won't you be here for the lockup and the Miranda readings? After all, you were the one who orchestrated the entire operation."

"No, I have something else to finish concerning the raid. But will you do me a big favor?"

"Sure, anything Brad."

"There are two men and a woman in the private cell. Kelly and Bob Walker and Marc Harper. Would you handle their release immediately? They're private prisoners, not charged with any crimes. They have been cooperative CI's. So it should be easy to release them. Just give them their personal effects and let them go. Please apologize on my behalf. Tell them, on my behalf, that it was necessary to hold them until the Mosque raid was over and successful. Their incarceration guaranteed that they would be safe and not be charged with any claims dealing with their participation of laundering money for Diric Omar. Also tell them that I made sure that they were documented confidential CI's and they can keep all of the money they received during the scheme, tax free. Hopefully that will help their attitude once you release them. I am sure you will find some very irritated people. Don't take it personally. Blame it on me."

"10-4 boss."

When the FBI guard opened the private holding cell and told the three friends that they were free to go, as well as relaying Brad Carr's message to them, Kelly went ballistic. Marc and Bob tried to calm her down, but she wanted to see Brad. The guard told Kelly that Brad was not coming to the holding cells that night when the prisoners came in. But he suggested that the three pick up their personal effects and go home. He assured them that there would not be a record of their incarceration or the fact that they were confidential CI's for the FBI. The guard suggested that they just needed to go back to their normal lives. He thanked them for their service to their Country. Kelly just gave the guard her middle finger and the three left to go to their homes, take a shower and sleep for a week. Marc was hopeful that his wife was understanding about what he had been doing over the last few years. He hadn't even been able to call her. She had called the police, but they were unable to locate Marc. It took her some time, but she finally understood once she heard the whole story.

Brad arrived at the International airport an hour before his plane would lift off to Europe. He had only a carryon with him. He would buy everything else he needed once he arrived in Switzerland. He hadn't calculated the total amount that he and Harrison would divide equally, but he knew it was north of four hundred million dollars. Enough to never be found by any authorities. Brad used one of his fake passports and his fake boarding pass to go through TSA security at the airport. He filled in his required forms that all passengers flying outside the United States were required to give to the TSA. Brad had two years to make up, and memorize, all of his and Harrison's information for their multiple identities. He was sure Harrison memorized his information also. All that information had been provided to Harrison over a year ago.

Once through security, Brad walked to the gate. As he approached the gate, he saw Harrison there. He was relieved. Harrison must have also done his homework on his new identities.

"Hey Harrison. Glad to see you. We have been waiting for this for a long time. In less than an hour, we'll be on our way to start our new lives."

"How did the raid go?" asked Harrison.

"Like clockwork. The FBI has hours of evidence on tape for every one of those arrested. It will take them several days to process everyone. They won't know I'm gone for at least a day."

"Are you sure that your supervisor, or someone from the FBI, will want to know why you didn't finish the sting, or even show up for their imprisonment?"

"Harrison, I have been working undercover for almost 9 years. I have had my life threatened, been beaten up, shot at multiple times, including twice when I was shot. I have never been able to have any kind of a relationship with any non-criminal woman for any normal period of time. I have lied, and been lied to, for so long that I'm not really sure what the real truths are anymore. I need this. I am owed this new life. I also don't want to do this all by myself. I want to share it with you. We have been friends for a long time. There have been long periods of time that we didn't communicate or see each other, but you have always been on my mind and a good friend."

As Harrison listened to Brad, he almost felt sorry for him. He was sure that Brad meant what he had said. As Brad was finishing his explanation of why he was committing this sting against his employer, Harrison started to notice TSA agents slowly escorting passengers and airline employees out of the international terminal. Brad was oblivious to what was happening around him. He was thinking about his future and the new fabulous life he would be living.

As the terminal became more and more vacant, Brad looked Harrison directly in his eyes and said, "What have you done?"

"Brad, I understand what you are telling me about your life over the last 9 years. Believe me, I get it. But you are stealing money from individual Somali business and individual people trying to live a better life as well as from US citizens and businesses. It's not the FBI's money. This is your fantasy life. I can't do this. I can't leave my family or friends"

Ted Taylor, Darius Clarke, David Scrivens and 4 Somali undercover FBI agents were walking toward the gate, guns drawn.

"Brad, get on your knees and put your hands above your head," yelled Ted Taylor, the FBI agent in charge of the Minneapolis office as he and his officers were walking towards Brad and Harrison.

"You turned me in?" said Brad to Harrison with great contempt.

Harrison nodded his head up and down and started to walk away from the gate.

Then Brad opened his carry on and took out a plastic box, opened it and took out a gun. It was an all polymer high grade plastic gun that was made by a 3-D copier at the Minneapolis FBI office. It had 5 plastic rounds each filled with gun powder. As an undercover agent, Brad needed a weapon that couldn't be detected by x-rays or metal detectors. The range of the rounds was only 15 feet, but they could be deadly.

Brad grabbed Harrison by the neck and put the plastic gun to the bottom of his chin. This was pure instinct on the part of Brad. Over the last 9 years he had been in situations that he wasn't sure how they would end. But Brad always survived. However this time, in his gut, he knew there was no way he was going to get out of this situation.

"You shouldn't have done this Harrison. You always had an out. I told you that we were friends. I would have understood if you said no to the sting. Our conversations were confidential. I would never have done this to you. Why?"

Harrison said nothing.

"Give it up Brad. You're too smart for this type of action. Put down the weapon and everyone gets out of here alive," said Ted.

Brad looked at Harrison and asked him, "Don't you have anything to say?"

Harrison looked at Brad and still said nothing. As the FBI agents were getting closer to Brad, they were still yelling for Brad to put down his weapon. The terminal was now completely empty. Brad was starting to get scared. It had been a long time since Brad had been scared. 9 years of undercover duty changes people. Brad was a completely changed man.

He had forgotten what scared felt like. The walls of the terminal were closing in on him. He panicked. He pushed Harrison away from him, turned the gun to his ear and pulled the trigger. The noise was slight, but the plastic bullet was deadly. Brad fell to the floor of the terminal bleeding from his head. Harrison turned away and ran behind the FBI agents. David Scrivens ran to Brad and put two fingers on his neck to feel for a pulse. He looked up at the other agents and just shook his head.

Harrison Ramsey stayed at the Downtown Minneapolis Marriott Hotel for several more days. He had contacted his supervisor at Marriott's headquarters in downtown Bethesda, Maryland several weeks after Brad and he had their first conversation about the sting against the FBI. Harrison's employer consented to have him work with the FBI. He could take off as much time as needed during the stings. His job in Aruba would be held open for him when the stings were concluded.

There were only a handful of people at Brad Carr's funeral several days after he killed himself. Only his FBI supervisor and several other FBI officials attended. No one from his family attended. He had not spoken to any of his family for over 9 years. Harrison, Kelly, Bob and Marc and his wife were all there. Diric Omar also attended. He was a free man just as his agreement indicated. Kelly and Marc didn't know if they should speak with Omar or spit in his face. Harrison and Bob actually shook hands with him and chatted for a few minutes. They knew it would be the last time they would ever see him again.

Brad was buried in a pine box. The funeral director at Memorial Gardens presided. David Scrivens said a few words on all of the good work Brad had done over his years at the FBI. He articulated that it was a sad day when Brad died. He understood what a long time undercover goes through and what it does to some agents. Even good ones. The funeral only lasted 30 minutes.

The night of Brad's funeral, Harrison, Bob and Kelly and Marc and his wife got together for dinner at the Downtown Marriott Hotel's Aurora Restaurant & Bar. The dinner was paid for by the government. They discussed every aspect of the last 2 plus years and vowed to always remain friends. There was a lot of tears and even some laughs. But, all of them had agreed that the last 2 plus years had made them all different people. Not for the bad, but more mature and compassionate. They each promised to always stay in touch. The next day all of them went back to their jobs with a new attitude knowing that their 2 year nightmare was finally finished.

After Harrison returned to Aruba, he called Alle Theil to have dinner with him. He told her all about the raid and Brad's sting against the FBI. That was the beginning of a close relationship. They started dating. Over the next years, Alle never mentioned anything about the circumstances of Johm Ruiz's death or the reasons she was involved. Harrison never mentioned the circumstances of the suicide of Jan Fingal. Both wondered about the circumstances of those deaths, but their relationship became too important. They married a year later. Bob and Kelly and Marc and his wife attended. Alle's entire family, from International Falls, took their first trip out of Minnesota to attend. It was a wonderful event with over 125 guests at the Aruba Marriott Hotel & Casino banquet room. Kelly's parents were there babysitting their 6 month old daughter. Bob and Kelly enjoyed their usual room on the eighth floor. Marc and his wife stayed on the eighth floor curtesy of Harrison. Marc had been promoted to varsity football coach and was optimistic that someday he would win a state championship.

Detective George Franken, who had been promoted to Chief of Police for the Island, attended with his wife. Chief Peterson retired and he and his wife also had a good time at the event. Kaydra was the maid of honor for the bride. She was working at the Costa Linda Beach Resort, as a trainee for the assistant food and beverage manager for their four restaurants and bars. Natasha Ruiz was invited but only stayed for two days. Kaydra and her mother spoke for over an hour and each promised to meet somewhere in the States in a few months.

It was an event that brought old friends even closer. The celebration lasted a whole week. Not one person who attended the event mentioned the names Brad Carr or Diric Omar the entire week of that wonderful reunion and celebration.

PGIL2023USA